# GEORGE O'CONNOR

# APOLLO
## THE BRILLIANT ONE

A NEAL PORTER BOOK

First Second
New York

"O MUSE! SING IN ME, AND THROUGH ME TELL A STORY."
—HOMER, THE ODYSSEY

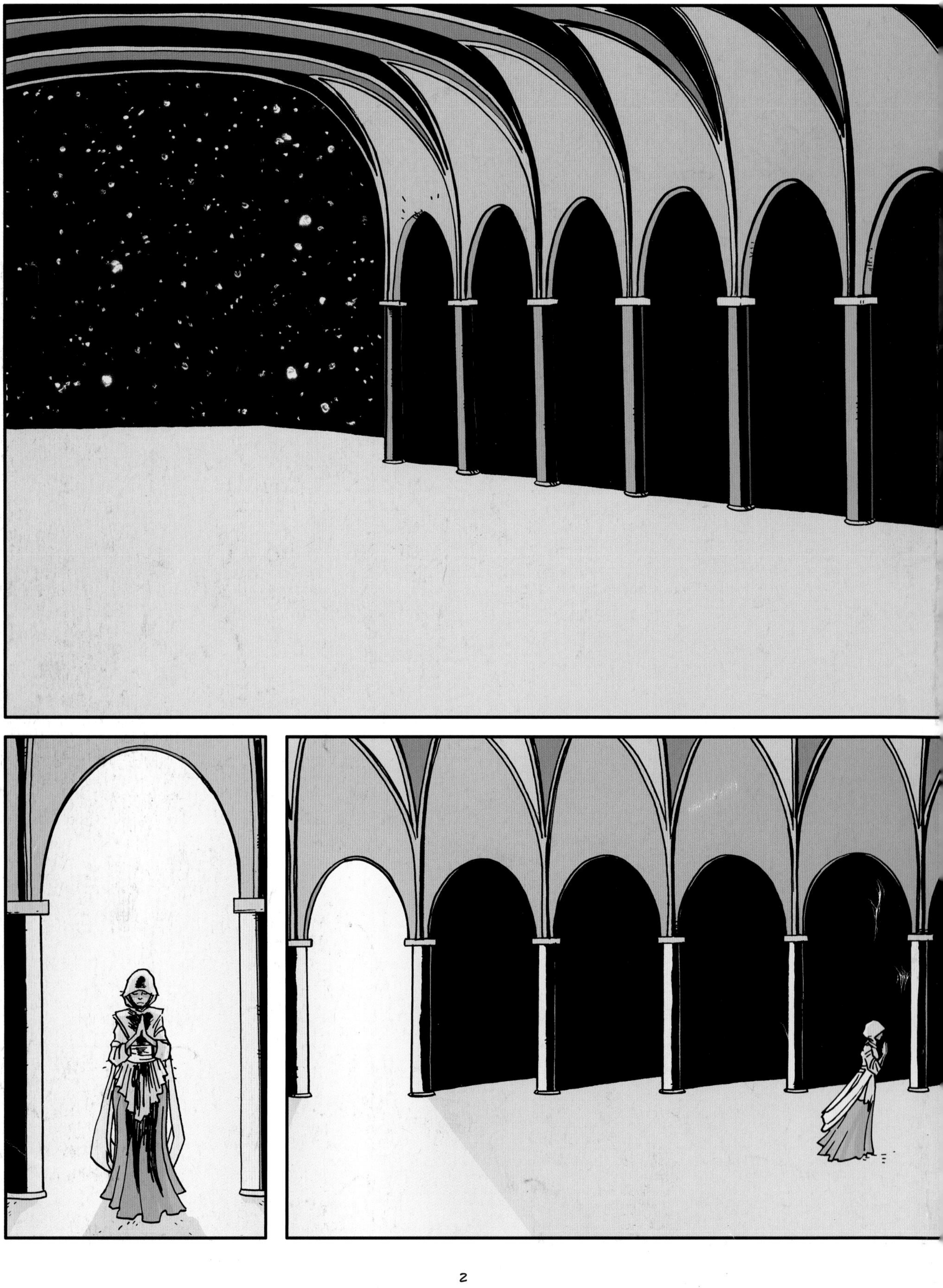

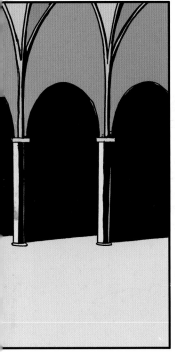

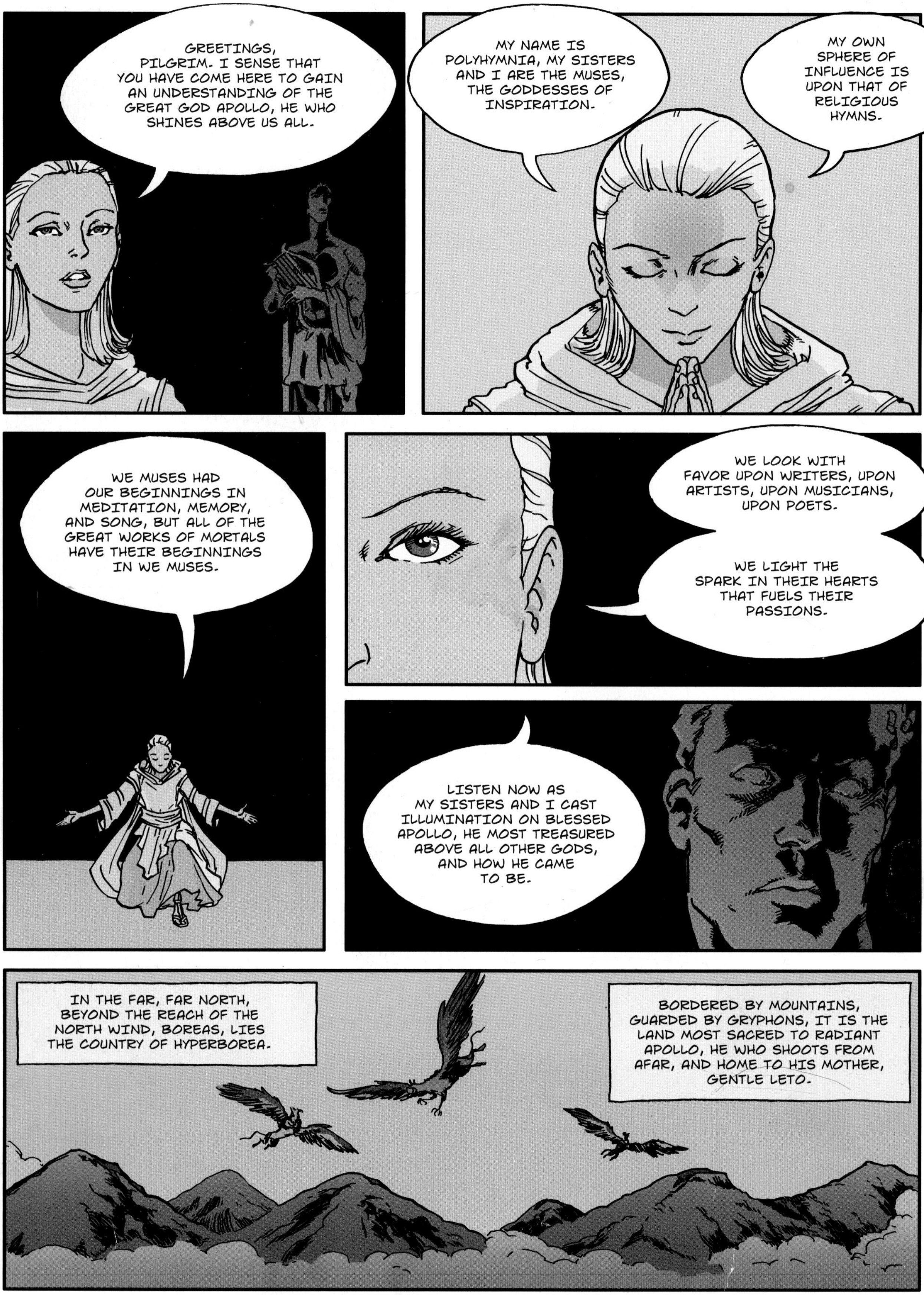
GREETINGS, PILGRIM. I SENSE THAT YOU HAVE COME HERE TO GAIN AN UNDERSTANDING OF THE GREAT GOD APOLLO, HE WHO SHINES ABOVE US ALL.
MY NAME IS POLYHYMNIA, MY SISTERS AND I ARE THE MUSES, THE GODDESSES OF INSPIRATION.
MY OWN SPHERE OF INFLUENCE IS UPON THAT OF RELIGIOUS HYMNS.
WE MUSES HAD OUR BEGINNINGS IN MEDITATION, MEMORY, AND SONG, BUT ALL OF THE GREAT WORKS OF MORTALS HAVE THEIR BEGINNINGS IN WE MUSES.
WE LOOK WITH FAVOR UPON WRITERS, UPON ARTISTS, UPON MUSICIANS, UPON POETS.
WE LIGHT THE SPARK IN THEIR HEARTS THAT FUELS THEIR PASSIONS.
LISTEN NOW AS MY SISTERS AND I CAST ILLUMINATION ON BLESSED APOLLO, HE MOST TREASURED ABOVE ALL OTHER GODS, AND HOW HE CAME TO BE.
IN THE FAR, FAR NORTH, BEYOND THE REACH OF THE NORTH WIND, BOREAS, LIES THE COUNTRY OF HYPERBOREA.
BORDERED BY MOUNTAINS, GUARDED BY GRYPHONS, IT IS THE LAND MOST SACRED TO RADIANT APOLLO, HE WHO SHOOTS FROM AFAR, AND HOME TO HIS MOTHER, GENTLE LETO.

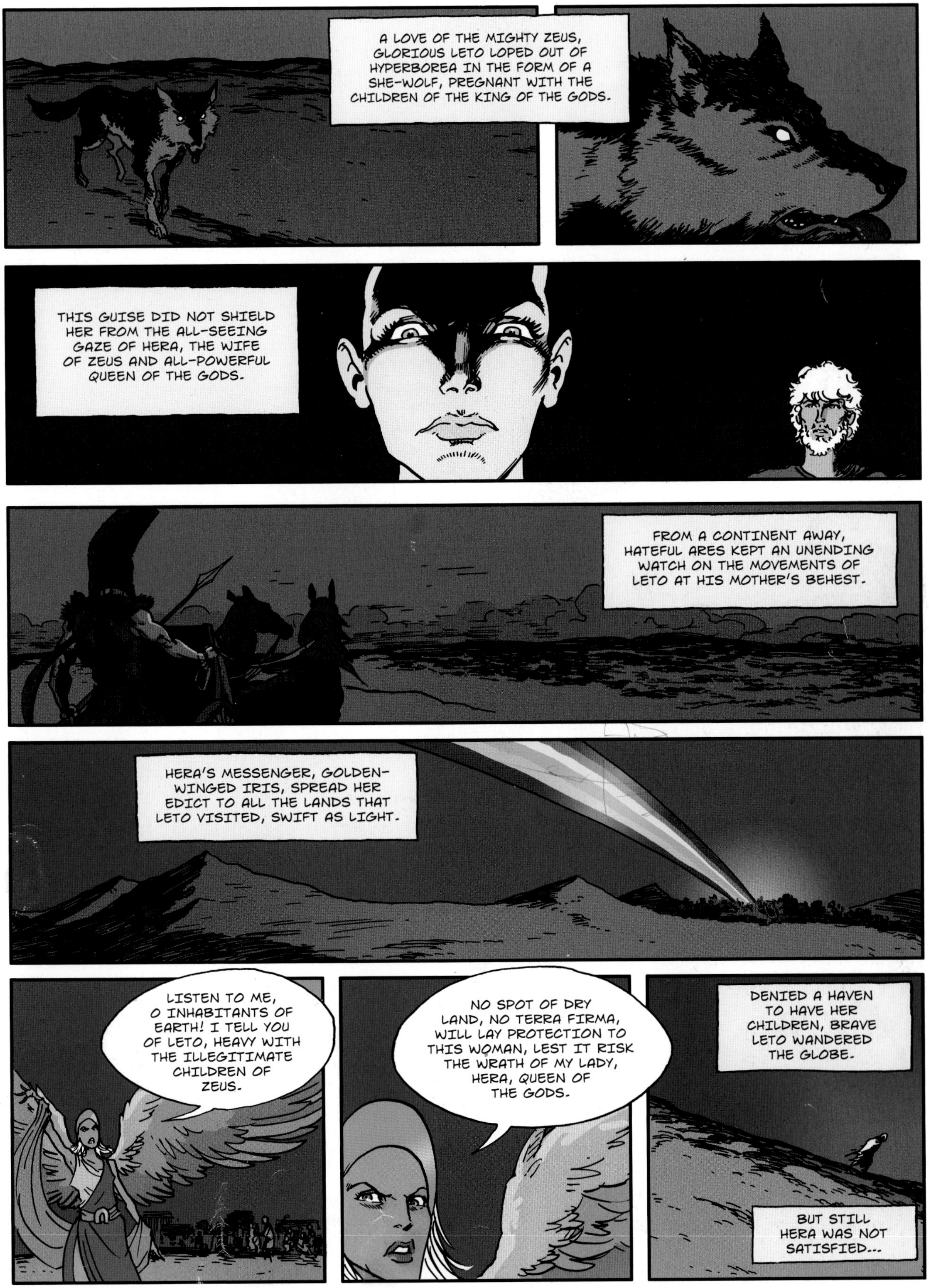
A LOVE OF THE MIGHTY ZEUS, GLORIOUS LETO LOPED OUT OF HYPERBOREA IN THE FORM OF A SHE-WOLF, PREGNANT WITH THE CHILDREN OF THE KING OF THE GODS.
THIS GUISE DID NOT SHIELD HER FROM THE ALL-SEEING GAZE OF HERA, THE WIFE OF ZEUS AND ALL-POWERFUL QUEEN OF THE GODS.
FROM A CONTINENT AWAY, HATEFUL ARES KEPT AN UNENDING WATCH ON THE MOVEMENTS OF LETO AT HIS MOTHER'S BEHEST.
HERA'S MESSENGER, GOLDEN-WINGED IRIS, SPREAD HER EDICT TO ALL THE LANDS THAT LETO VISITED, SWIFT AS LIGHT.
LISTEN TO ME, O INHABITANTS OF EARTH! I TELL YOU OF LETO, HEAVY WITH THE ILLEGITIMATE CHILDREN OF ZEUS.
NO SPOT OF DRY LAND, NO TERRA FIRMA, WILL LAY PROTECTION TO THIS WOMAN, LEST IT RISK THE WRATH OF MY LADY, HERA, QUEEN OF THE GODS.
DENIED A HAVEN TO HAVE HER CHILDREN, BRAVE LETO WANDERED THE GLOBE.
BUT STILL HERA WAS NOT SATISFIED...

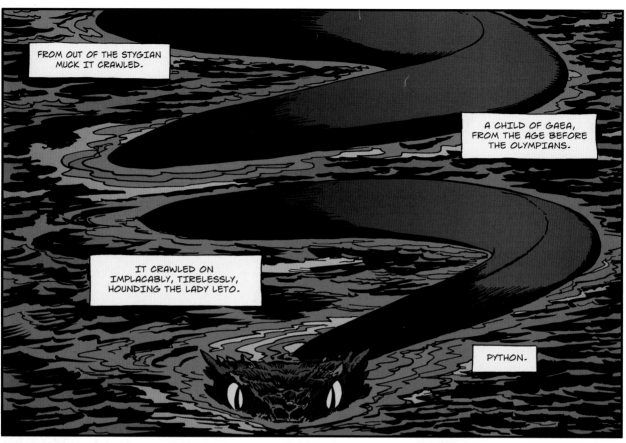

FROM OUT OF THE STYGIAN MUCK IT CRAWLED.

A CHILD OF GAEA, FROM THE AGE BEFORE THE OLYMPIANS.

IT CRAWLED ON IMPLACABLY, TIRELESSLY, HOUNDING THE LADY LETO.

PYTHON.

HERA SET THIS MONSTER ON THE HEELS OF LETO.

UNABLE TO STOP, UNABLE TO REST, LETO KEPT MOVING, CONSTANTLY.

ZEUS TOOK PITY ON HIS FORMER LOVER, CARRYING HIS UNBORN CHILDREN.

HE DARED NOT DIRECTLY DISOBEY HERA'S EDICT OF NO TERRA FIRMA, BUT HE SENT OUT BOREAS TO HIS BROTHER, POSEIDON, WITH A REQUEST FOR HELP.

I HAVE GOT TO GET MY OWN MESSENGER.

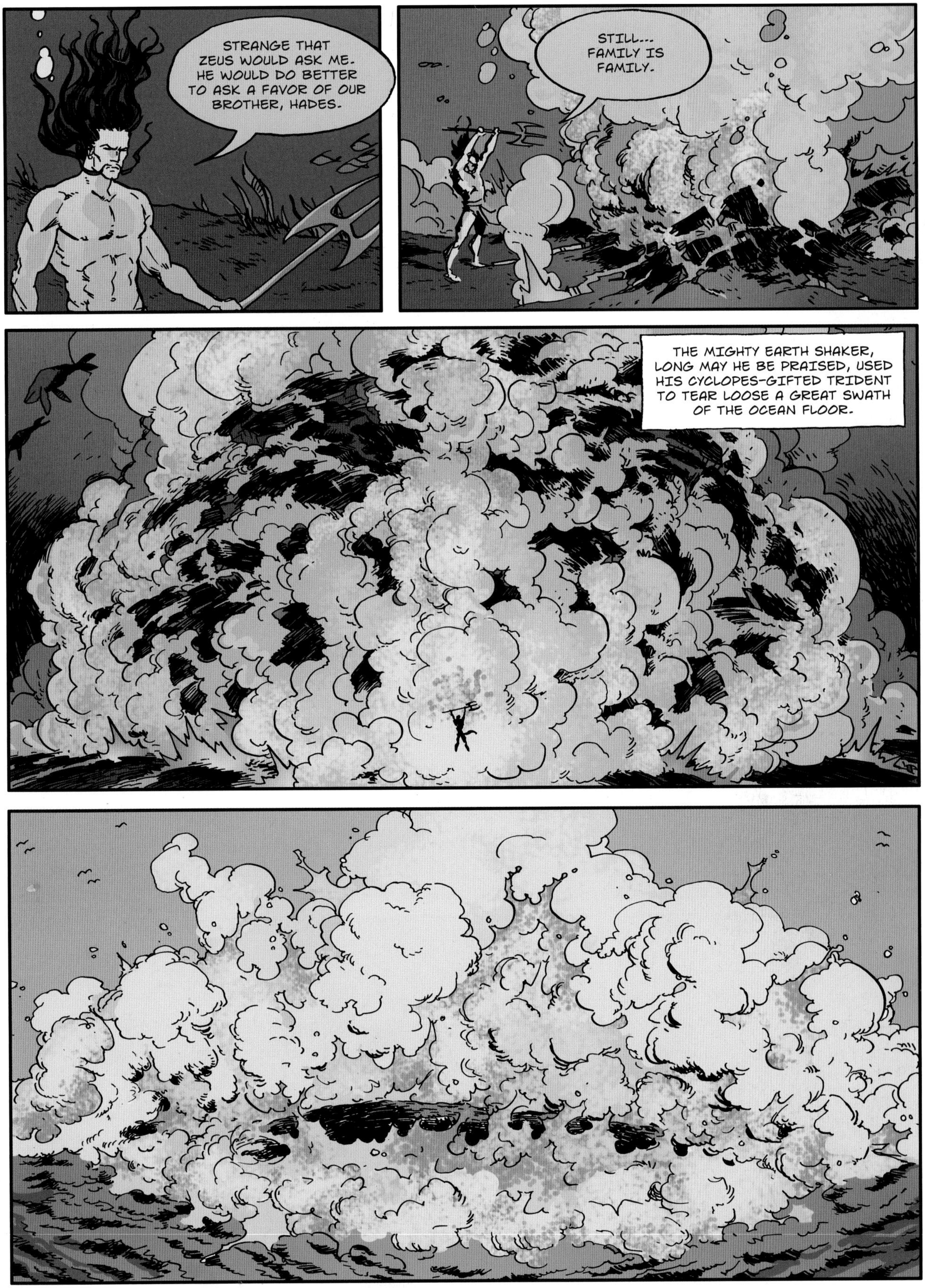
STRANGE THAT ZEUS WOULD ASK ME. HE WOULD DO BETTER TO ASK A FAVOR OF OUR BROTHER, HADES.
STILL... FAMILY IS FAMILY.
THE MIGHTY EARTH SHAKER, LONG MAY HE BE PRAISED, USED HIS CYCLOPES-GIFTED TRIDENT TO TEAR LOOSE A GREAT SWATH OF THE OCEAN FLOOR.

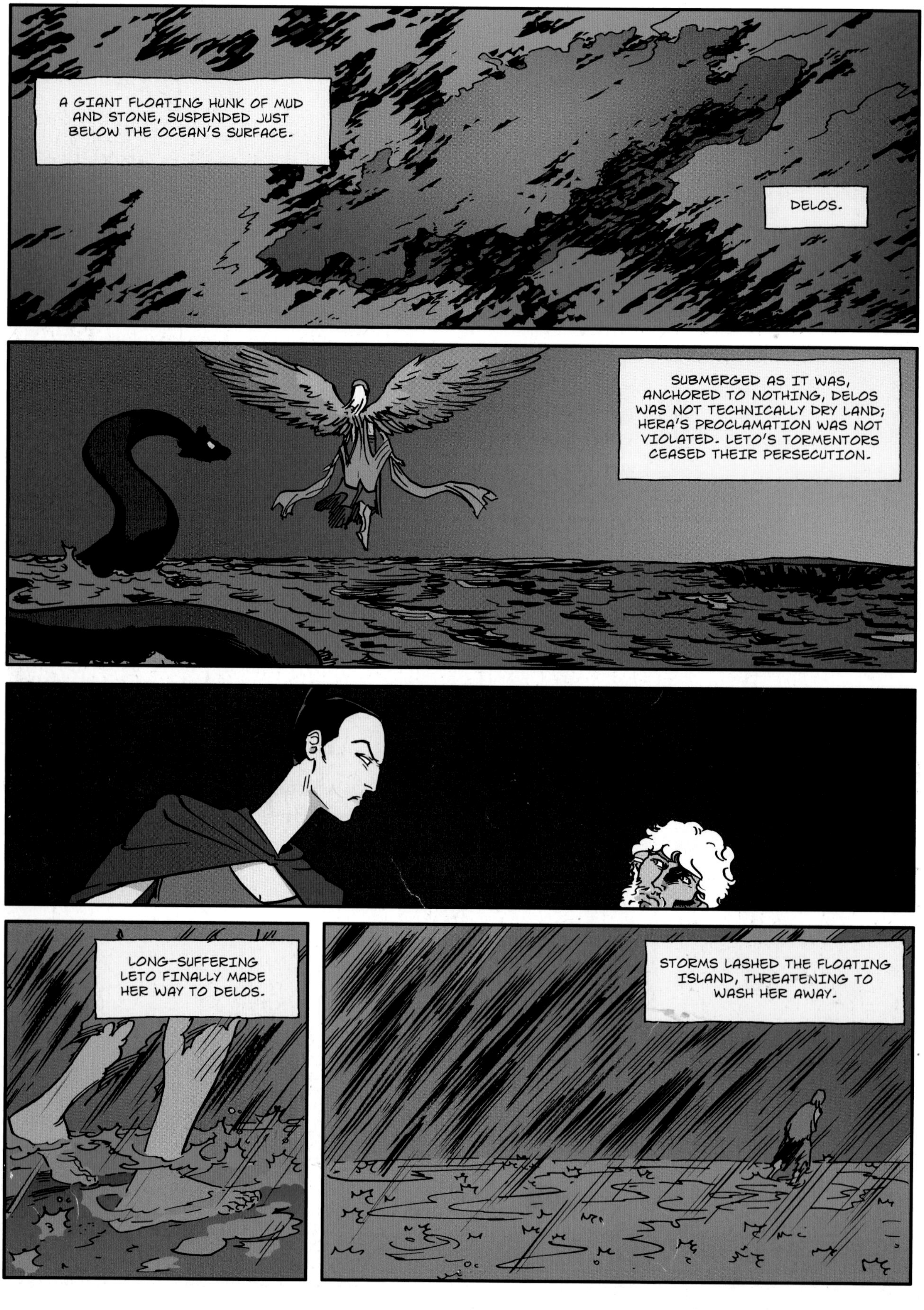
A GIANT FLOATING HUNK OF MUD AND STONE, SUSPENDED JUST BELOW THE OCEAN'S SURFACE.
DELOS.
SUBMERGED AS IT WAS, ANCHORED TO NOTHING, DELOS WAS NOT TECHNICALLY DRY LAND; HERA'S PROCLAMATION WAS NOT VIOLATED. LETO'S TORMENTORS CEASED THEIR PERSECUTION.
LONG-SUFFERING LETO FINALLY MADE HER WAY TO DELOS.
STORMS LASHED THE FLOATING ISLAND, THREATENING TO WASH HER AWAY.

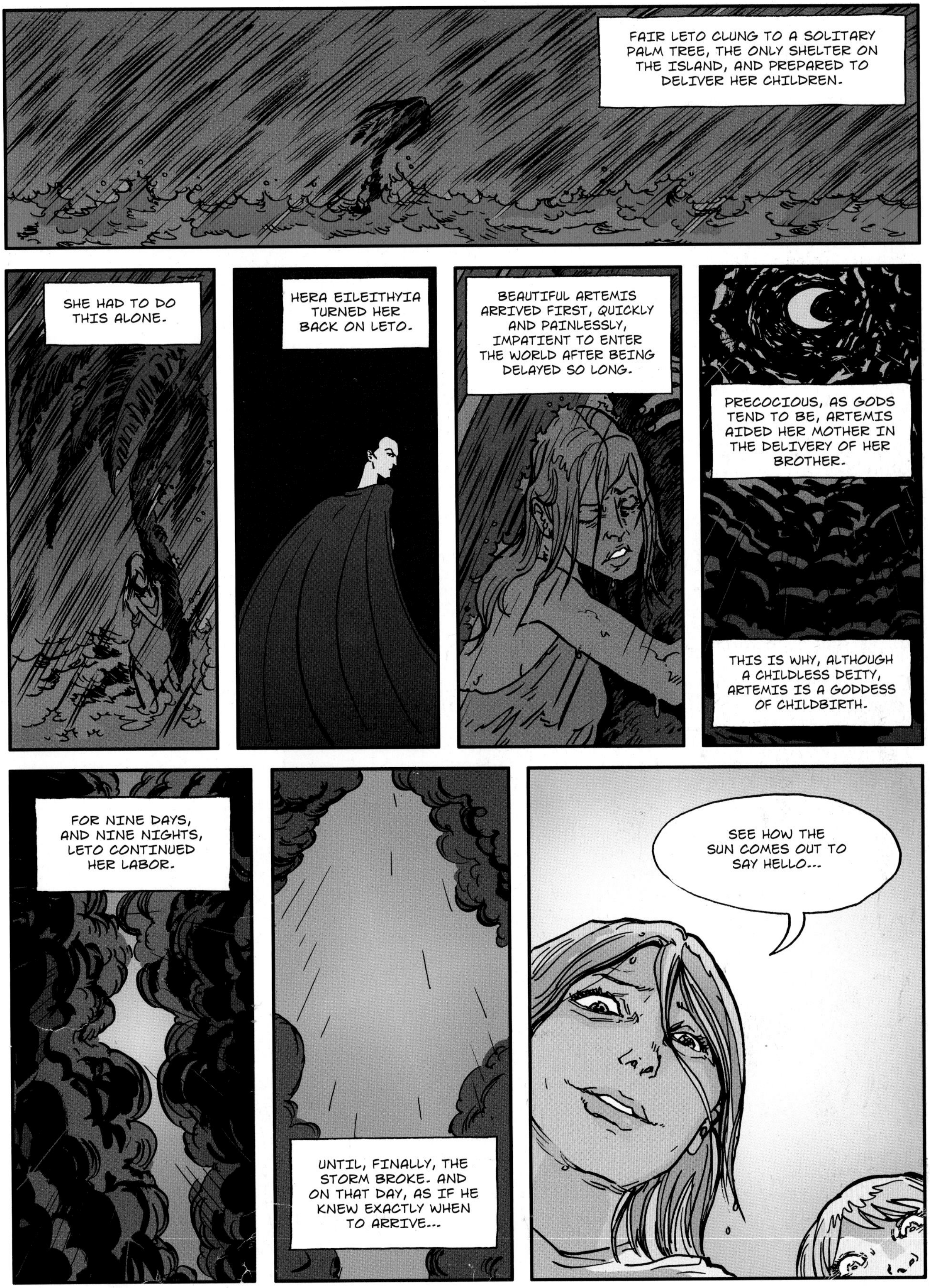
FAIR LETO CLUNG TO A SOLITARY PALM TREE, THE ONLY SHELTER ON THE ISLAND, AND PREPARED TO DELIVER HER CHILDREN.
SHE HAD TO DO THIS ALONE.
HERA EILEITHYIA TURNED HER BACK ON LETO.
BEAUTIFUL ARTEMIS ARRIVED FIRST, QUICKLY AND PAINLESSLY, IMPATIENT TO ENTER THE WORLD AFTER BEING DELAYED SO LONG.
PRECOCIOUS, AS GODS TEND TO BE, ARTEMIS AIDED HER MOTHER IN THE DELIVERY OF HER BROTHER.
THIS IS WHY, ALTHOUGH A CHILDLESS DEITY, ARTEMIS IS A GODDESS OF CHILDBIRTH.
FOR NINE DAYS, AND NINE NIGHTS, LETO CONTINUED HER LABOR.
UNTIL, FINALLY, THE STORM BROKE. AND ON THAT DAY, AS IF HE KNEW EXACTLY WHEN TO ARRIVE...
SEE HOW THE SUN COMES OUT TO SAY HELLO...

MY PRECIOUS BABY APOLLO.

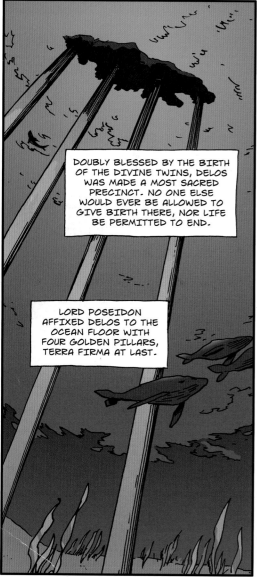

DOUBLY BLESSED BY THE BIRTH OF THE DIVINE TWINS, DELOS WAS MADE A MOST SACRED PRECINCT. NO ONE ELSE WOULD EVER BE ALLOWED TO GIVE BIRTH THERE, NOR LIFE BE PERMITTED TO END.

LORD POSEIDON AFFIXED DELOS TO THE OCEAN FLOOR WITH FOUR GOLDEN PILLARS, TERRA FIRMA AT LAST.

LETO'S PERSECUTION ENDED, BOREAS ARRIVED WITH AN INVITATION FOR HER AND THE TWINS.

TO LIVE ON MOUNT OLYMPUS, THE TALLEST MOUNTAIN LEFT STANDING AFTER THE WAR OF TITANS AND GODS, AS HONORED GUESTS.

THERE BLESSED APOLLO AND ARTEMIS WERE PRESENTED BEFORE THEIR FATHER, CLOUD-GATHERING ZEUS, FOR THE FIRST TIME.

PROUD ZEUS ASKED HIS CHILDREN WHAT GIFTS THEY DESIRED, WHAT THEY WOULD BECOME.

FAIR ARTEMIS WENT FIRST:

SHE WANTED TO REMAIN UNMARRIED FOREVER; TO HUNT GAME WITH A SILVER BOW AND ARROWS; TO RUN WILD THROUGH THE WOODS AND MOUNTAINS WITH HER OWN ENTOURAGE OF OCEANIDES, NYMPHS, AND HOUNDS.

ZEUS GAVE HER ALL SHE ASKED FOR AND MORE.

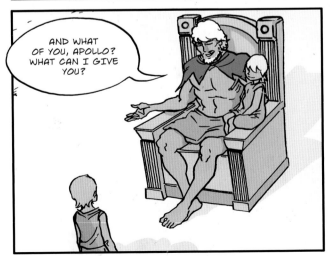

AND WHAT OF YOU, APOLLO? WHAT CAN I GIVE YOU?

APOLLO DIDN'T ANSWER.

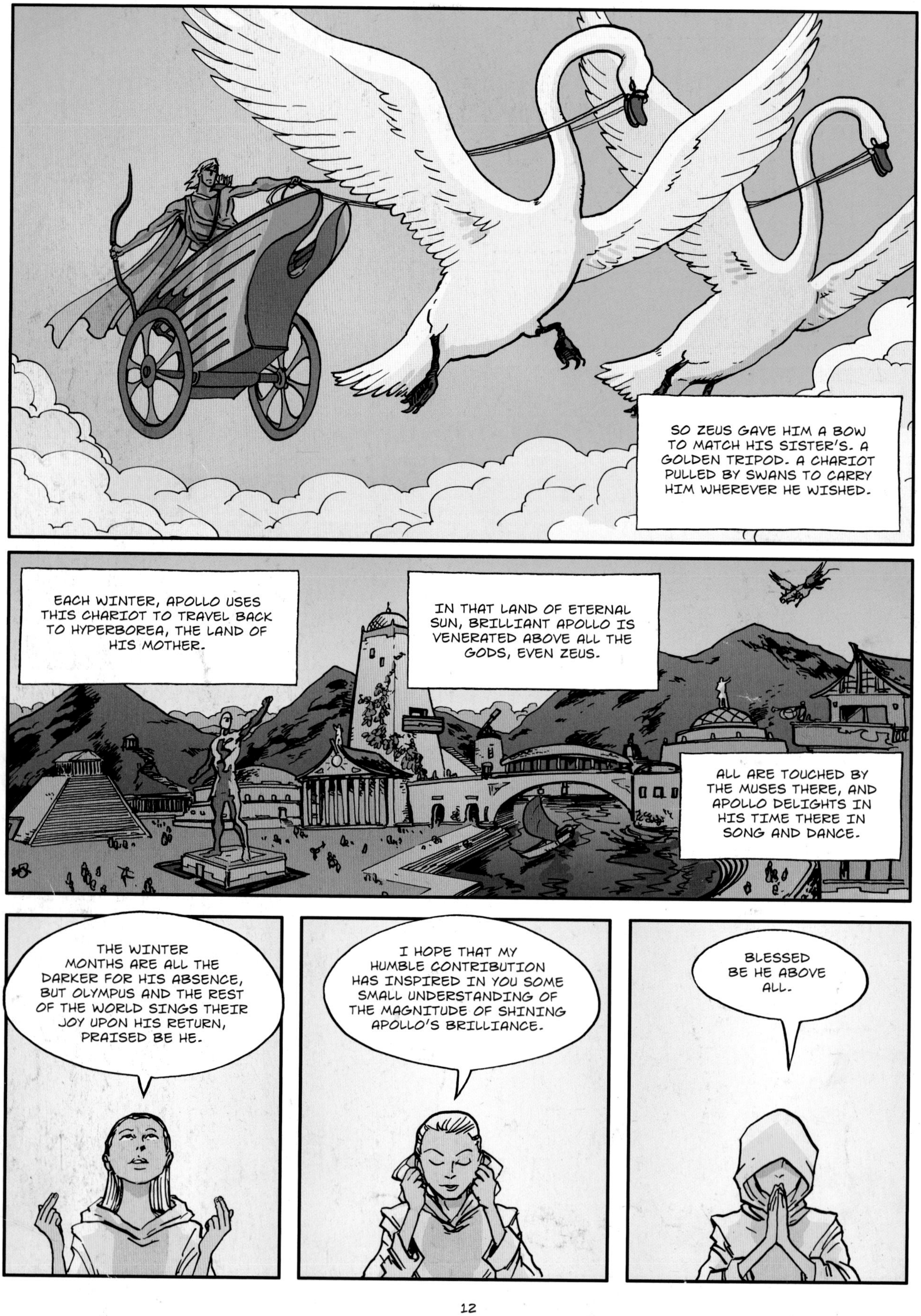
SO ZEUS GAVE HIM A BOW TO MATCH HIS SISTER'S. A GOLDEN TRIPOD. A CHARIOT PULLED BY SWANS TO CARRY HIM WHEREVER HE WISHED.
EACH WINTER, APOLLO USES THIS CHARIOT TO TRAVEL BACK TO HYPERBOREA, THE LAND OF HIS MOTHER.
IN THAT LAND OF ETERNAL SUN, BRILLIANT APOLLO IS VENERATED ABOVE ALL THE GODS, EVEN ZEUS.
ALL ARE TOUCHED BY THE MUSES THERE, AND APOLLO DELIGHTS IN HIS TIME THERE IN SONG AND DANCE.
THE WINTER MONTHS ARE ALL THE DARKER FOR HIS ABSENCE, BUT OLYMPUS AND THE REST OF THE WORLD SINGS THEIR JOY UPON HIS RETURN, PRAISED BE HE.
I HOPE THAT MY HUMBLE CONTRIBUTION HAS INSPIRED IN YOU SOME SMALL UNDERSTANDING OF THE MAGNITUDE OF SHINING APOLLO'S BRILLIANCE.
BLESSED BE HE ABOVE ALL.

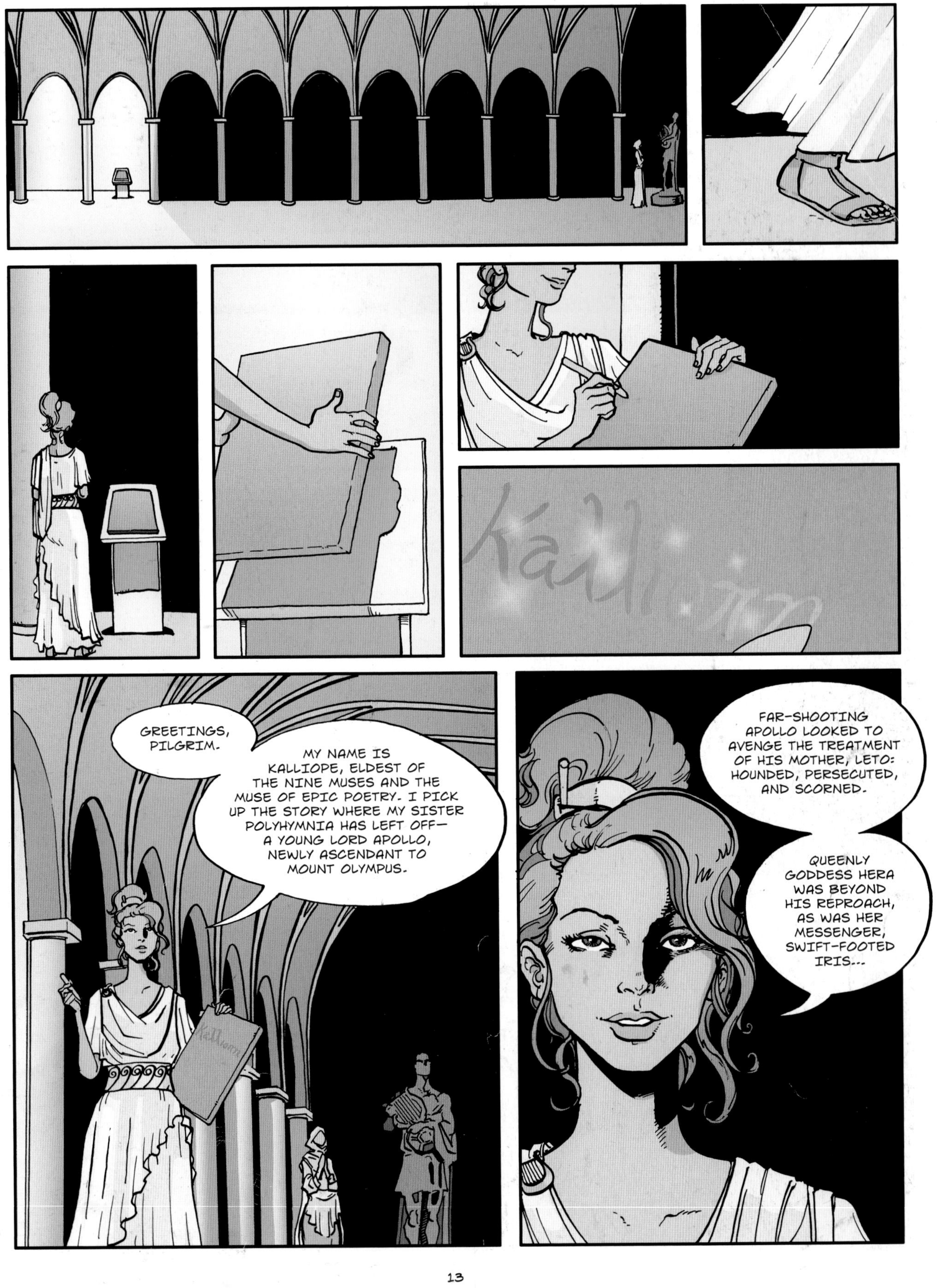
GREETINGS, PILGRIM.
MY NAME IS KALLIOPE, ELDEST OF THE NINE MUSES AND THE MUSE OF EPIC POETRY. I PICK UP THE STORY WHERE MY SISTER POLYHYMNIA HAS LEFT OFF— A YOUNG LORD APOLLO, NEWLY ASCENDANT TO MOUNT OLYMPUS.
FAR-SHOOTING APOLLO LOOKED TO AVENGE THE TREATMENT OF HIS MOTHER, LETO: HOUNDED, PERSECUTED, AND SCORNED.
QUEENLY GODDESS HERA WAS BEYOND HIS REPROACH, AS WAS HER MESSENGER, SWIFT-FOOTED IRIS...

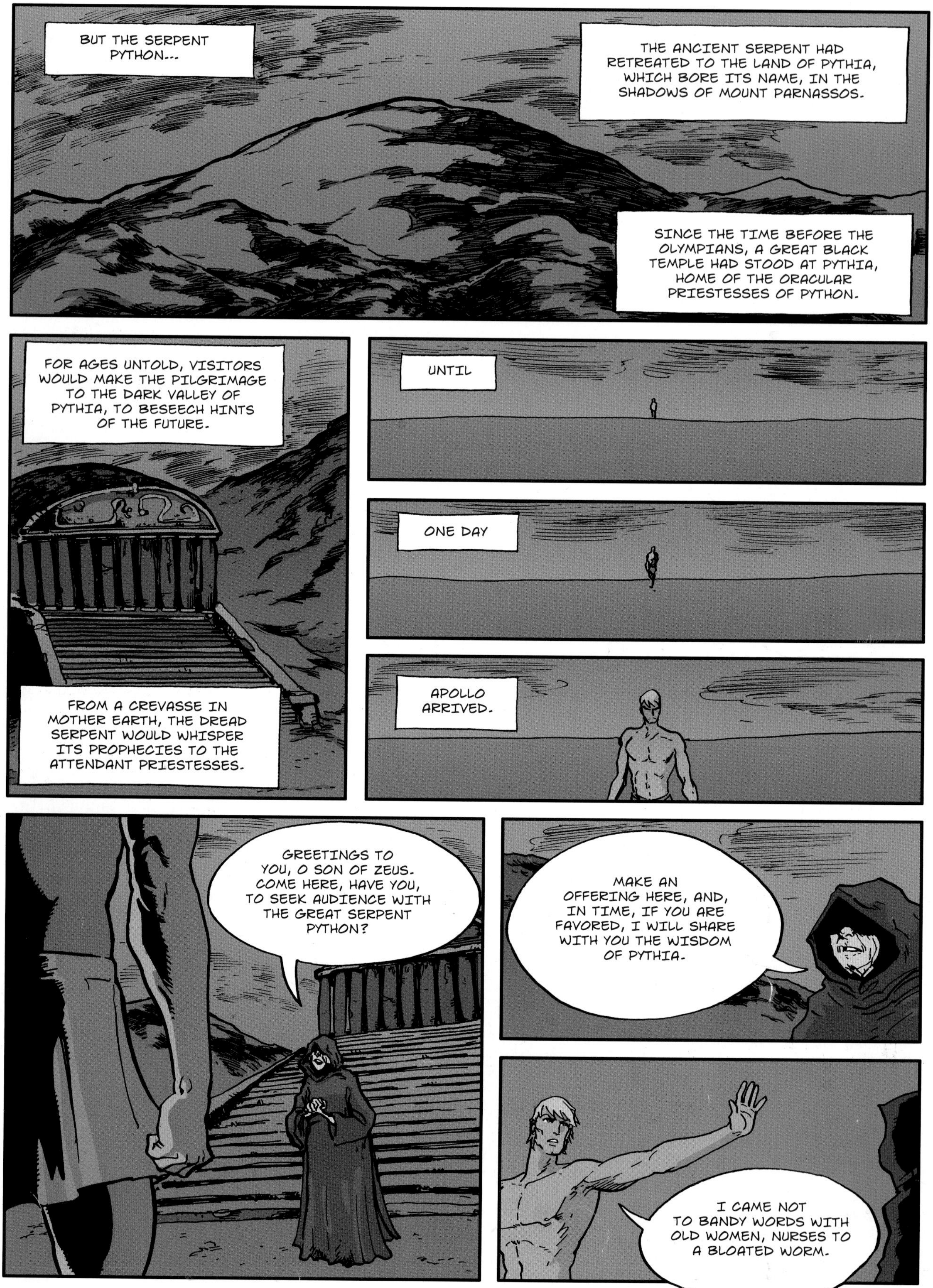

BUT THE SERPENT PYTHON...
THE ANCIENT SERPENT HAD RETREATED TO THE LAND OF PYTHIA, WHICH BORE ITS NAME, IN THE SHADOWS OF MOUNT PARNASSOS.
SINCE THE TIME BEFORE THE OLYMPIANS, A GREAT BLACK TEMPLE HAD STOOD AT PYTHIA, HOME OF THE ORACULAR PRIESTESSES OF PYTHON.
FOR AGES UNTOLD, VISITORS WOULD MAKE THE PILGRIMAGE TO THE DARK VALLEY OF PYTHIA, TO BESEECH HINTS OF THE FUTURE.
FROM A CREVASSE IN MOTHER EARTH, THE DREAD SERPENT WOULD WHISPER ITS PROPHECIES TO THE ATTENDANT PRIESTESSES.
UNTIL
ONE DAY
APOLLO ARRIVED.
GREETINGS TO YOU, O SON OF ZEUS. COME HERE, HAVE YOU, TO SEEK AUDIENCE WITH THE GREAT SERPENT PYTHON?
MAKE AN OFFERING HERE, AND, IN TIME, IF YOU ARE FAVORED, I WILL SHARE WITH YOU THE WISDOM OF PYTHIA.
I CAME NOT TO BANDY WORDS WITH OLD WOMEN, NURSES TO A BLOATED WORM.

I CAME TO ASK A QUESTION OF YOUR SICKLY MASTER, AND IT IS TO THE BLACK SERPENT DIRECTLY I SHALL ADDRESS IT.

HHHIIIIIISSSSSS...

IT IS NOT OFTEN THAT GREAT PYTHON ADDRESSES ONE DIRECTLY.

IT REMAINS TO BE SEEN IF YOU ARE FORTUNATE IN THAT REGARD...

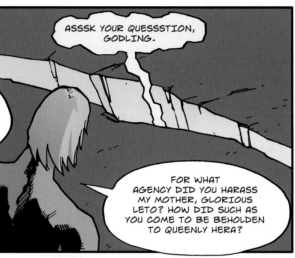

ASSSK YOUR QUESSSTION, GODLING.

FOR WHAT AGENCY DID YOU HARASS MY MOTHER, GLORIOUS LETO? HOW DID SUCH AS YOU COME TO BE BEHOLDEN TO QUEENLY HERA?

I AM FAR, FAR OLDER THAN THAT UPSSSTART, HERA; I OWE HER NO ALLEGIANCCCE.

A PROPHECCCCY TOLD ME I WOULD MEET MY END AT THE HANDSSS OF A CHILD OF LETO. THAT IS WHY I PURSSSUED HER.

TO BE HONESSST, I THOUGHT IT WOULD BE ARTEMISSSS WHO WOULD COME.

SHE SSSEEMSSS THE MORE FORMIDABLE.

YOU DABBLE IN PROPHECY? THIS IS MY FIRST PROGNOSTICATION, SERPENT.

YOU MEET YOUR END NOW.

BENEATH THE FAIR, SANDALED FEET OF APOLLO, GRANDMOTHER EARTH SHUDDERED.

SHINING APOLLO LEAPT—

—HIGHER AND HIGHER, AS THE GROUND RUSHED UP TO MEET HIM.

HHHHHHIIIIIISSSSSSSSSSS!!!

WE'LL SEE.

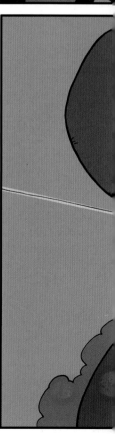

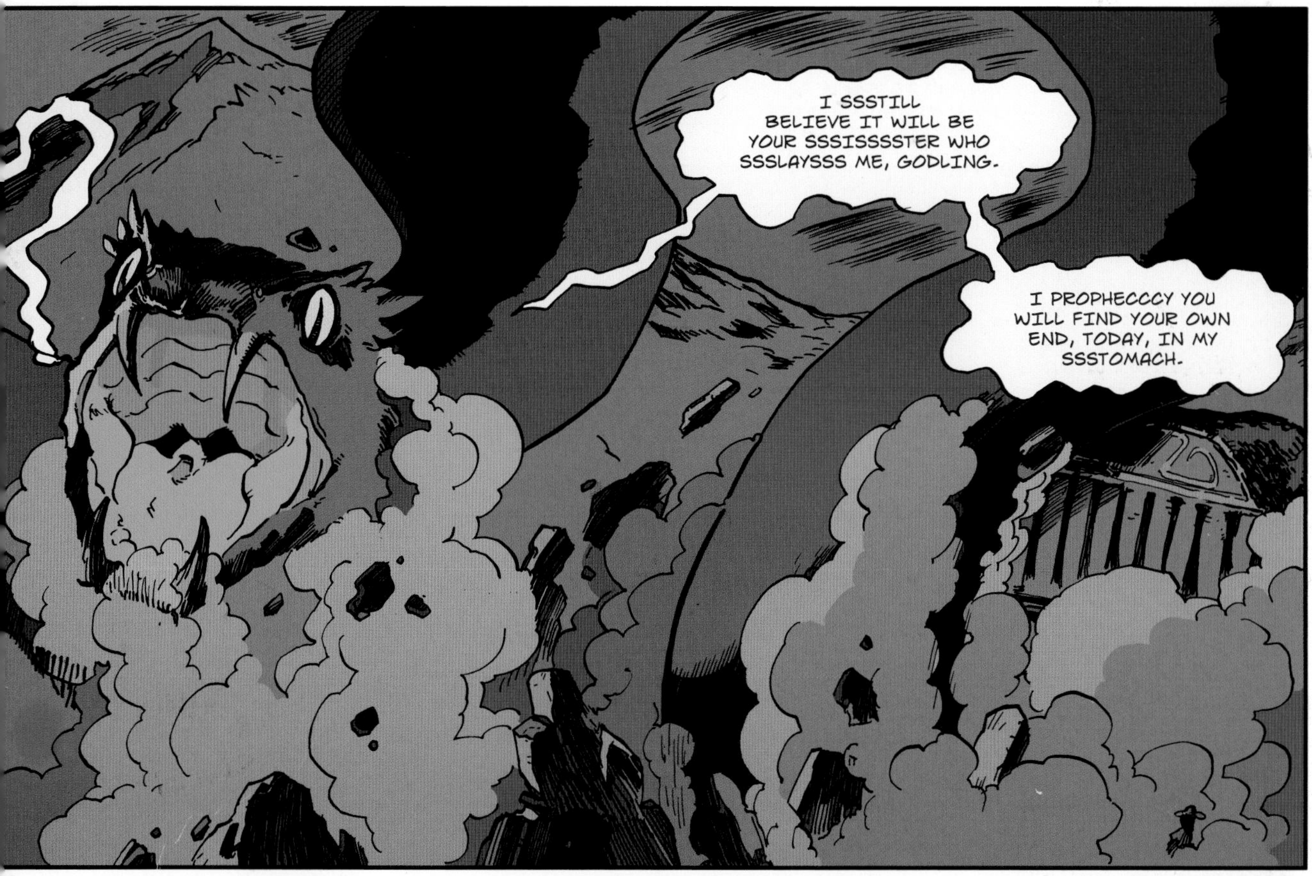
I SSSTILL BELIEVE IT WILL BE YOUR SSSISSSSSTER WHO SSSLAYSSS ME, GODLING.
I PROPHECCCY YOU WILL FIND YOUR OWN END, TODAY, IN MY SSSTOMACH.

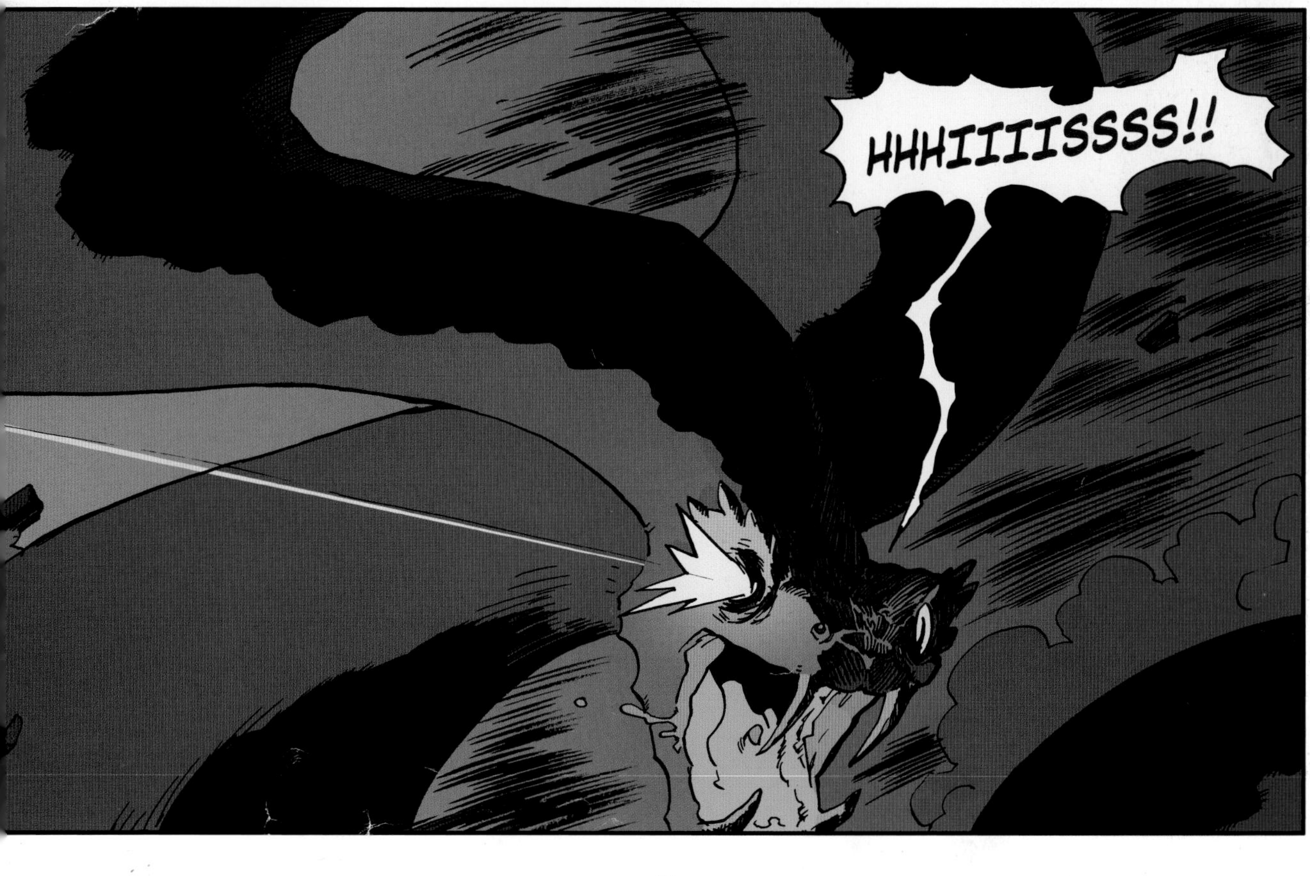
HHHIIIISSSS!!

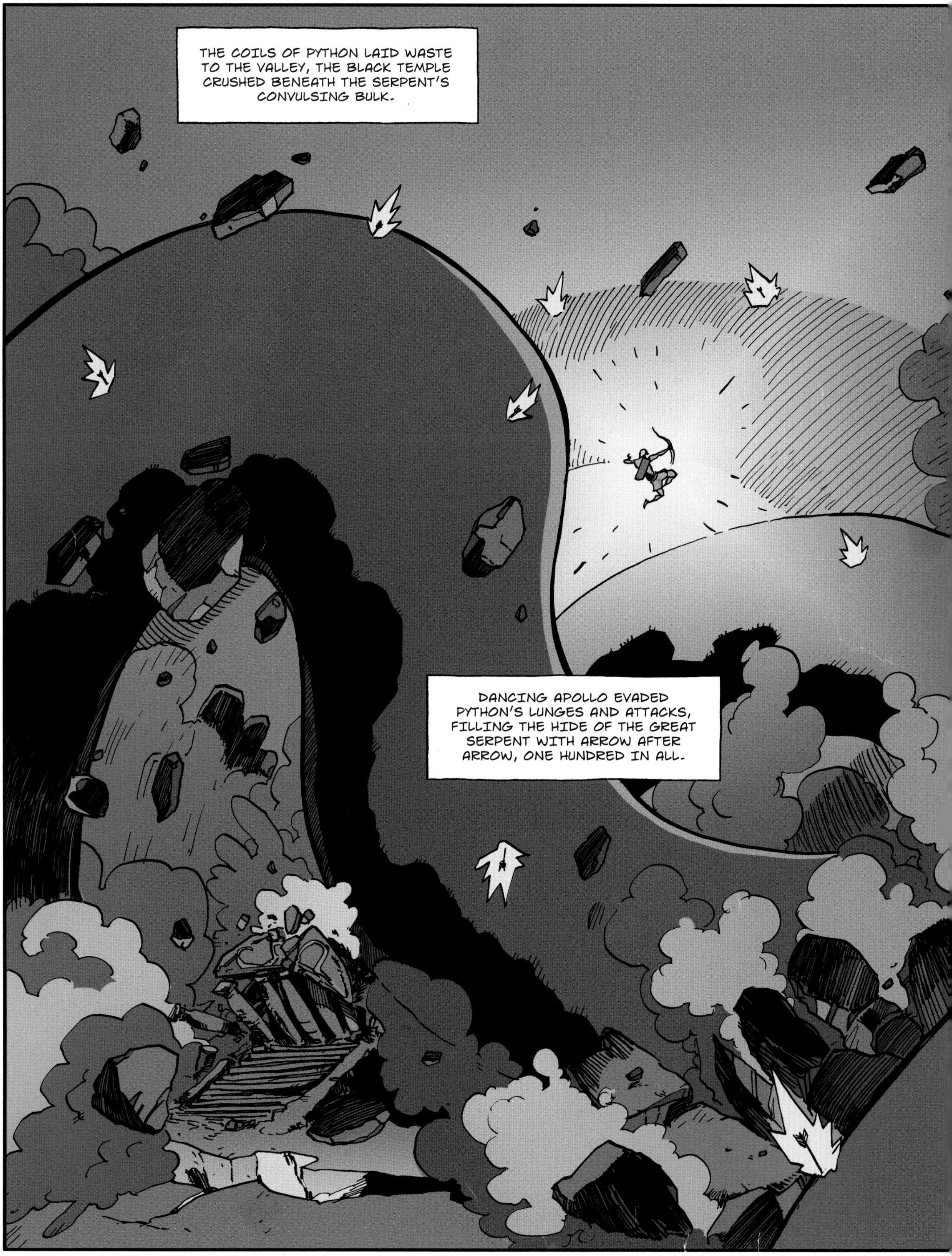
THE COILS OF PYTHON LAID WASTE TO THE VALLEY, THE BLACK TEMPLE CRUSHED BENEATH THE SERPENT'S CONVULSING BULK.
DANCING APOLLO EVADED PYTHON'S LUNGES AND ATTACKS, FILLING THE HIDE OF THE GREAT SERPENT WITH ARROW AFTER ARROW, ONE HUNDRED IN ALL.

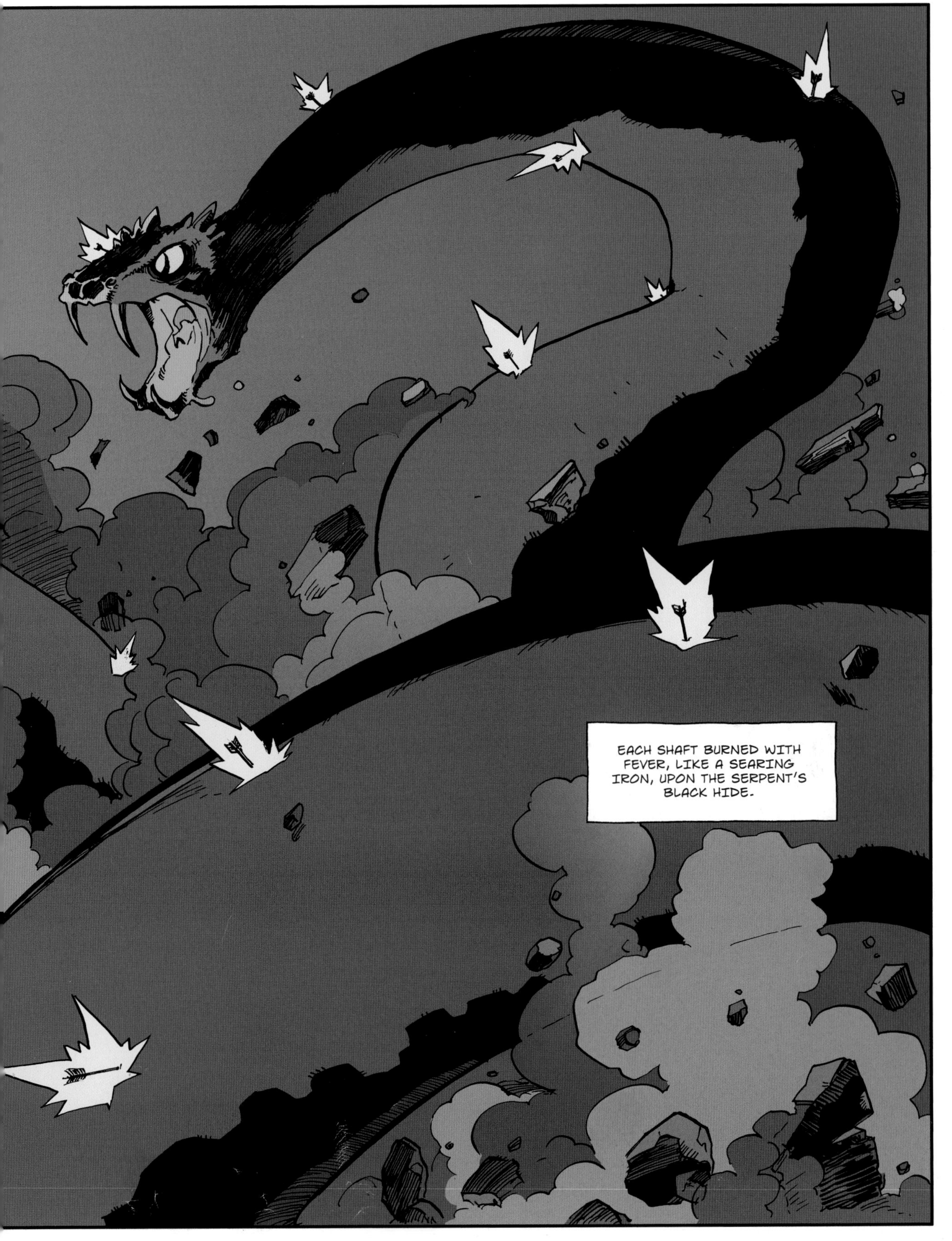
EACH SHAFT BURNED WITH FEVER, LIKE A SEARING IRON, UPON THE SERPENT'S BLACK HIDE.

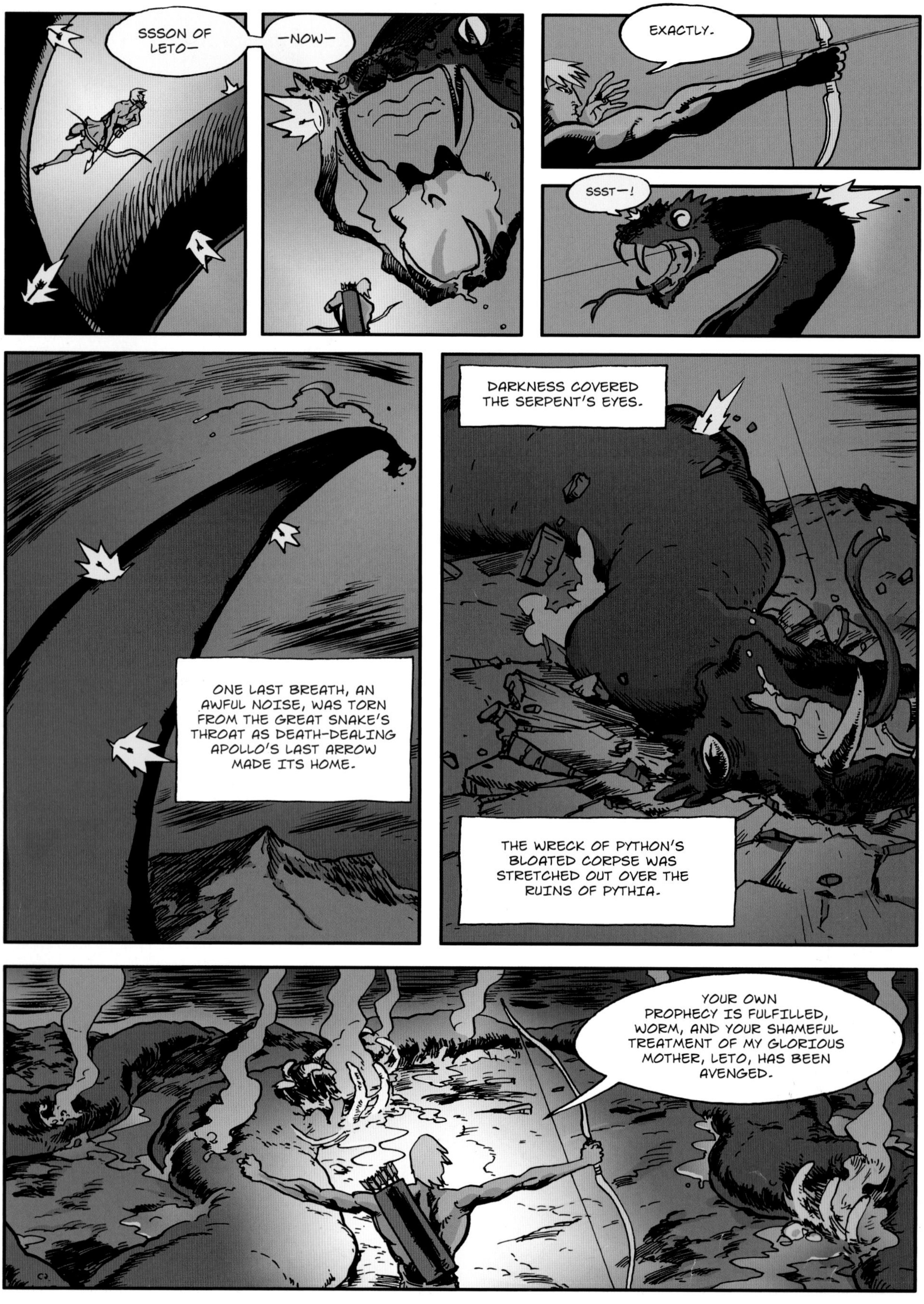
SSSON OF LETO—
—NOW—
EXACTLY.
SSST—!
ONE LAST BREATH, AN AWFUL NOISE, WAS TORN FROM THE GREAT SNAKE'S THROAT AS DEATH-DEALING APOLLO'S LAST ARROW MADE ITS HOME.
DARKNESS COVERED THE SERPENT'S EYES.
THE WRECK OF PYTHON'S BLOATED CORPSE WAS STRETCHED OUT OVER THE RUINS OF PYTHIA.
YOUR OWN PROPHECY IS FULFILLED, WORM, AND YOUR SHAMEFUL TREATMENT OF MY GLORIOUS MOTHER, LETO, HAS BEEN AVENGED.

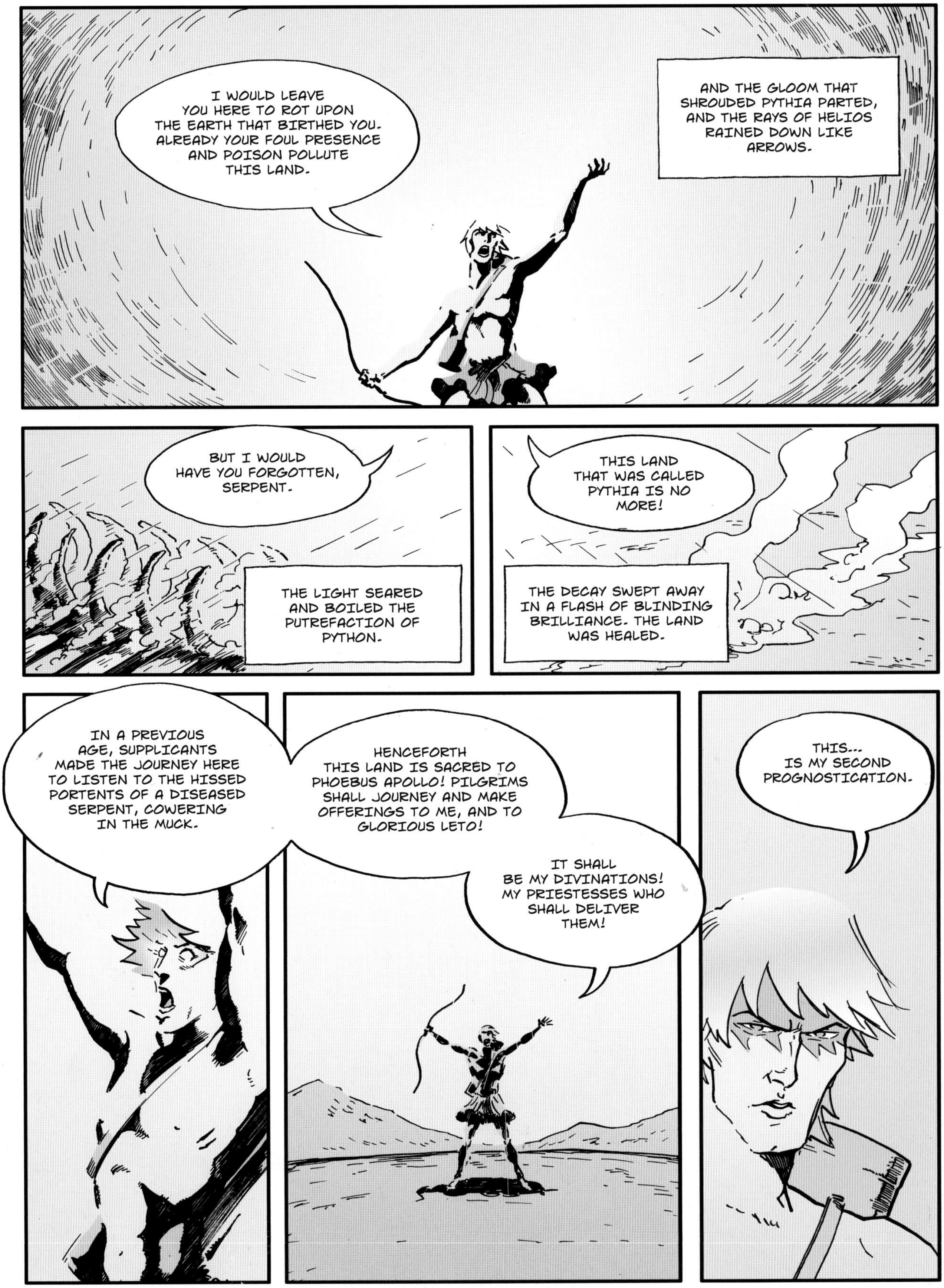
I WOULD LEAVE YOU HERE TO ROT UPON THE EARTH THAT BIRTHED YOU. ALREADY YOUR FOUL PRESENCE AND POISON POLLUTE THIS LAND.
AND THE GLOOM THAT SHROUDED PYTHIA PARTED, AND THE RAYS OF HELIOS RAINED DOWN LIKE ARROWS.
BUT I WOULD HAVE YOU FORGOTTEN, SERPENT.
THE LIGHT SEARED AND BOILED THE PUTREFACTION OF PYTHON.
THIS LAND THAT WAS CALLED PYTHIA IS NO MORE!
THE DECAY SWEPT AWAY IN A FLASH OF BLINDING BRILLIANCE. THE LAND WAS HEALED.
IN A PREVIOUS AGE, SUPPLICANTS MADE THE JOURNEY HERE TO LISTEN TO THE HISSED PORTENTS OF A DISEASED SERPENT, COWERING IN THE MUCK.
HENCEFORTH THIS LAND IS SACRED TO PHOEBUS APOLLO! PILGRIMS SHALL JOURNEY AND MAKE OFFERINGS TO ME, AND TO GLORIOUS LETO!
IT SHALL BE MY DIVINATIONS! MY PRIESTESSES WHO SHALL DELIVER THEM!
THIS... IS MY SECOND PROGNOSTICATION.

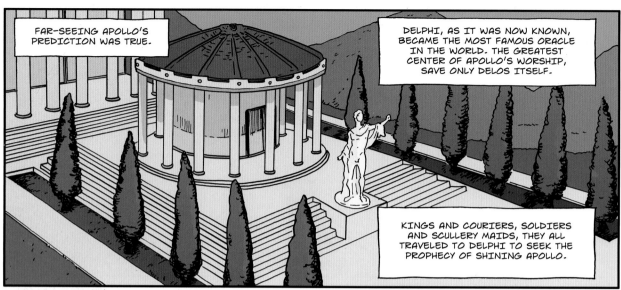

FAR-SEEING APOLLO'S PREDICTION WAS TRUE.

DELPHI, AS IT WAS NOW KNOWN, BECAME THE MOST FAMOUS ORACLE IN THE WORLD. THE GREATEST CENTER OF APOLLO'S WORSHIP, SAVE ONLY DELOS ITSELF.

KINGS AND COURIERS, SOLDIERS AND SCULLERY MAIDS, THEY ALL TRAVELED TO DELPHI TO SEEK THE PROPHECY OF SHINING APOLLO.

AH, WE ARE JOINED, POLYHYMNIA.

INTRODUCE YOURSELVES, SISTERS.

I AM THE MUSE EUTERPE. MINE IS THE REALM OF MUSIC AND LYRIC POETRY.

AND I AM TERPSICHORE, MUSE OF DANCE AND CHORAL SONG.

MY SISTER AND I WILL TELL YOU A STORY OF APOLLO, TOGETHER.

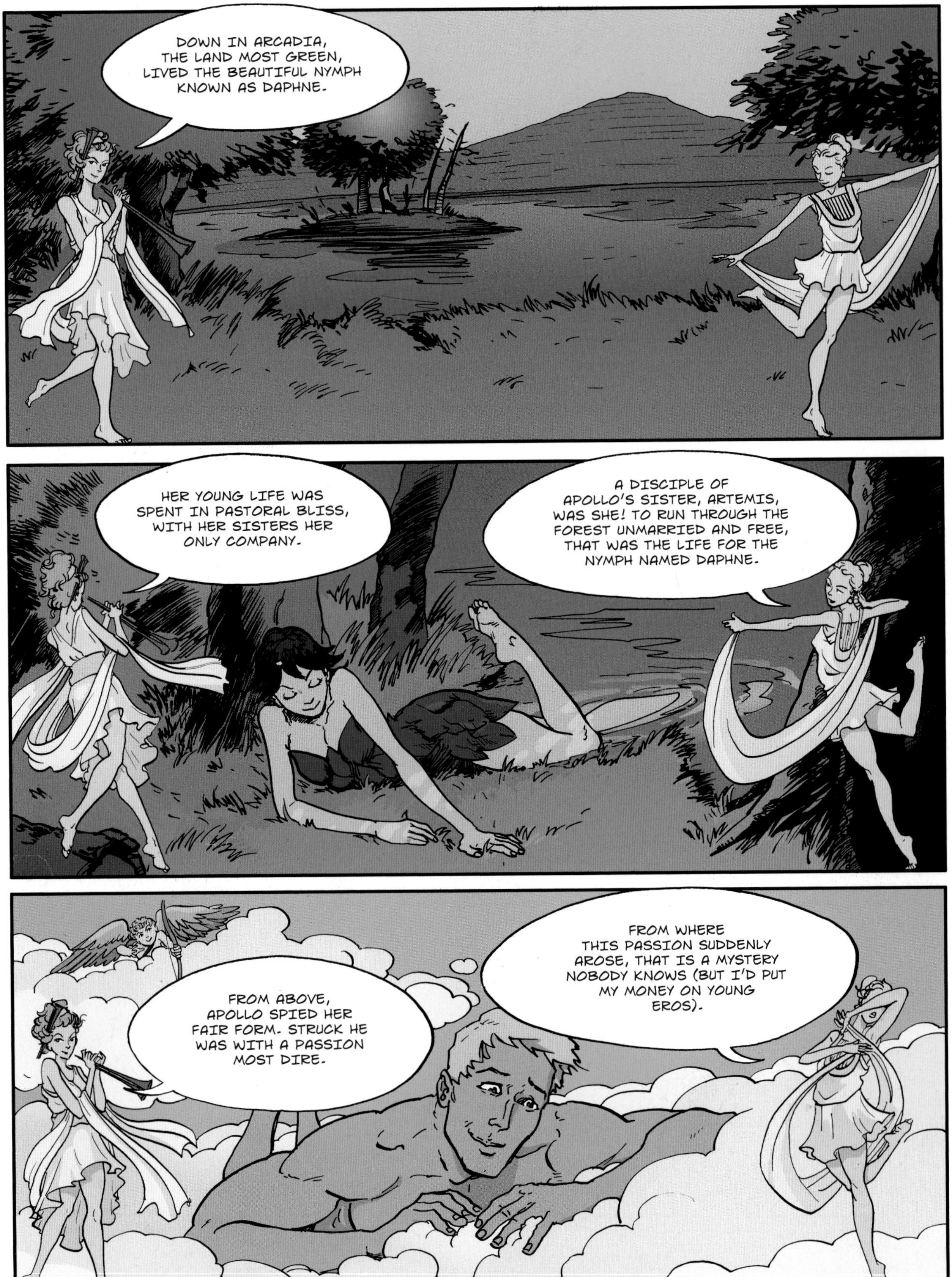
DOWN IN ARCADIA, THE LAND MOST GREEN, LIVED THE BEAUTIFUL NYMPH KNOWN AS DAPHNE.
HER YOUNG LIFE WAS SPENT IN PASTORAL BLISS, WITH HER SISTERS HER ONLY COMPANY.
A DISCIPLE OF APOLLO'S SISTER, ARTEMIS, WAS SHE! TO RUN THROUGH THE FOREST UNMARRIED AND FREE, THAT WAS THE LIFE FOR THE NYMPH NAMED DAPHNE.
FROM ABOVE, APOLLO SPIED HER FAIR FORM. STRUCK HE WAS WITH A PASSION MOST DIRE.
FROM WHERE THIS PASSION SUDDENLY AROSE, THAT IS A MYSTERY NOBODY KNOWS (BUT I'D PUT MY MONEY ON YOUNG EROS).

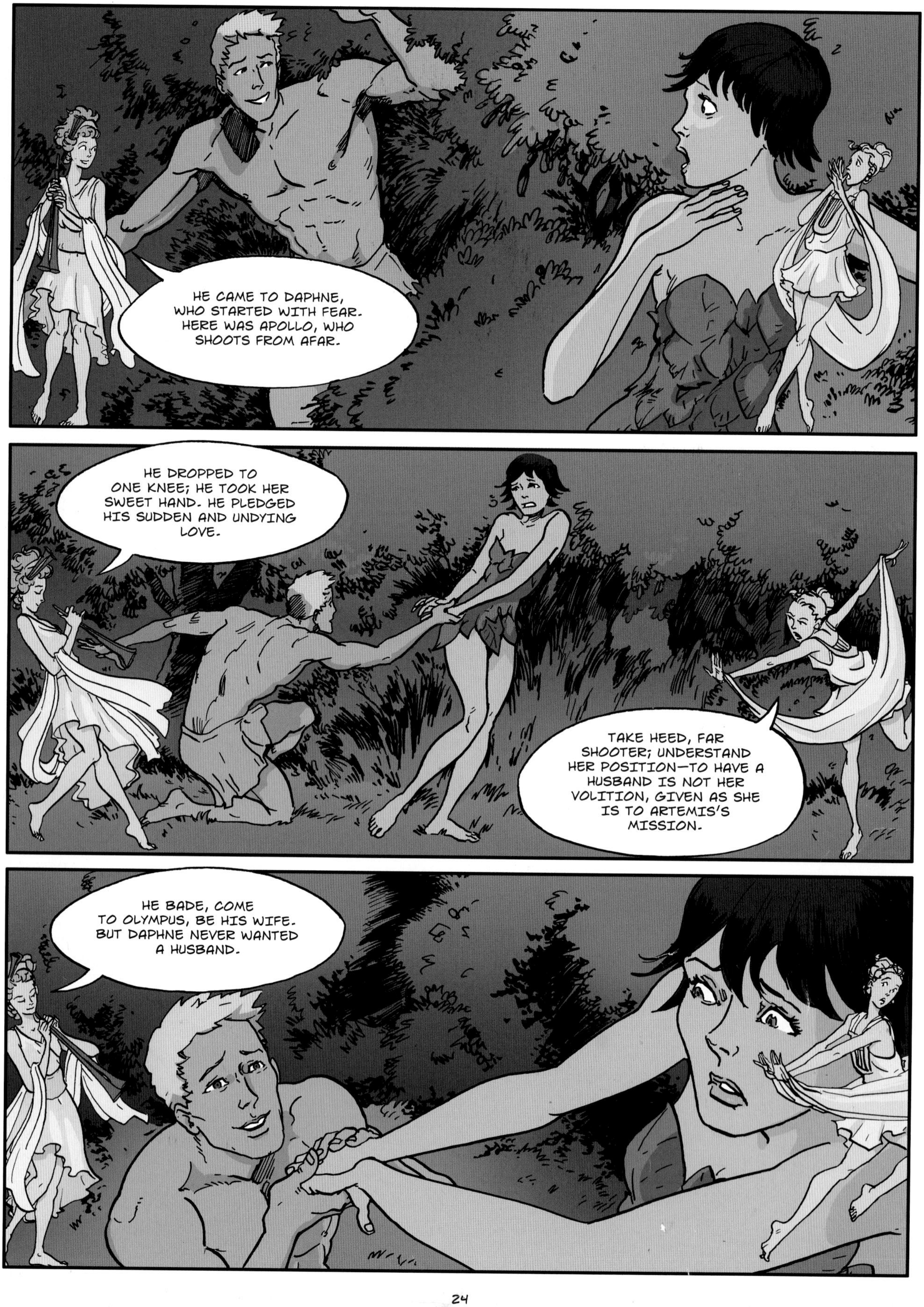
HE CAME TO DAPHNE, WHO STARTED WITH FEAR. HERE WAS APOLLO, WHO SHOOTS FROM AFAR.
HE DROPPED TO ONE KNEE; HE TOOK HER SWEET HAND. HE PLEDGED HIS SUDDEN AND UNDYING LOVE.
TAKE HEED, FAR SHOOTER; UNDERSTAND HER POSITION—TO HAVE A HUSBAND IS NOT HER VOLITION, GIVEN AS SHE IS TO ARTEMIS'S MISSION.
HE BADE, COME TO OLYMPUS, BE HIS WIFE. BUT DAPHNE NEVER WANTED A HUSBAND.

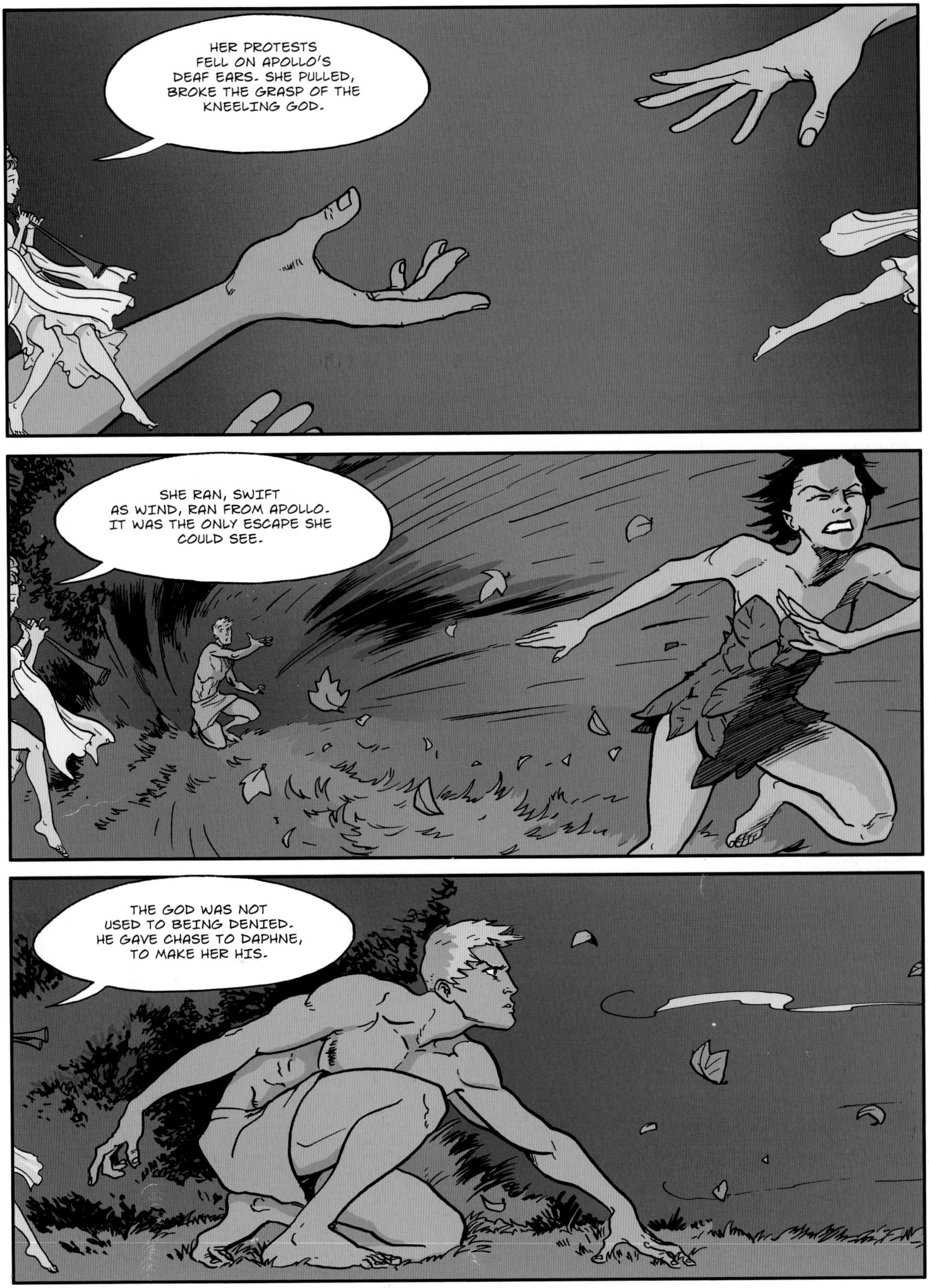
HER PROTESTS FELL ON APOLLO'S DEAF EARS. SHE PULLED, BROKE THE GRASP OF THE KNEELING GOD.
SHE RAN, SWIFT AS WIND, RAN FROM APOLLO. IT WAS THE ONLY ESCAPE SHE COULD SEE.
THE GOD WAS NOT USED TO BEING DENIED. HE GAVE CHASE TO DAPHNE, TO MAKE HER HIS.

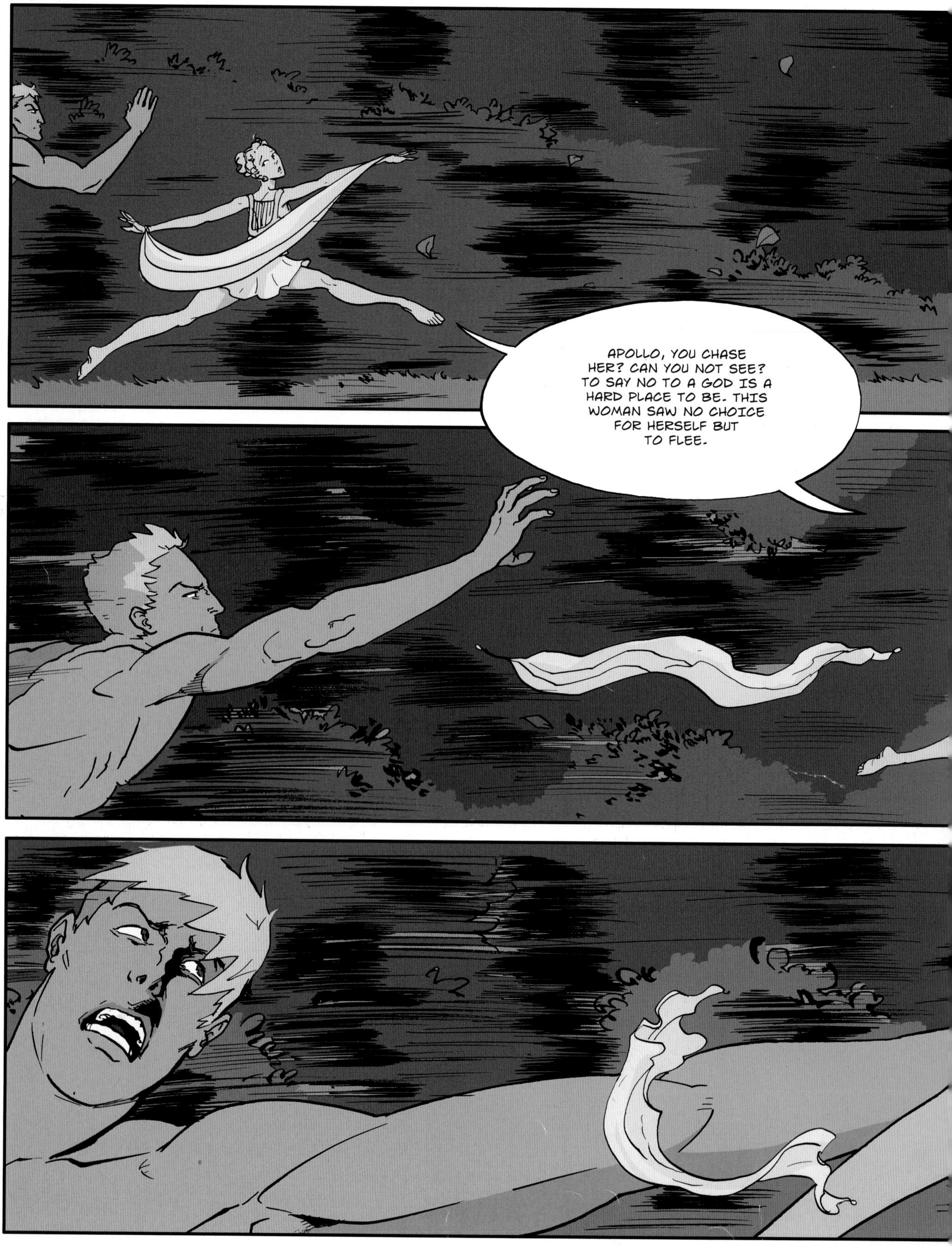
APOLLO, YOU CHASE HER? CAN YOU NOT SEE? TO SAY NO TO A GOD IS A HARD PLACE TO BE. THIS WOMAN SAW NO CHOICE FOR HERSELF BUT TO FLEE.

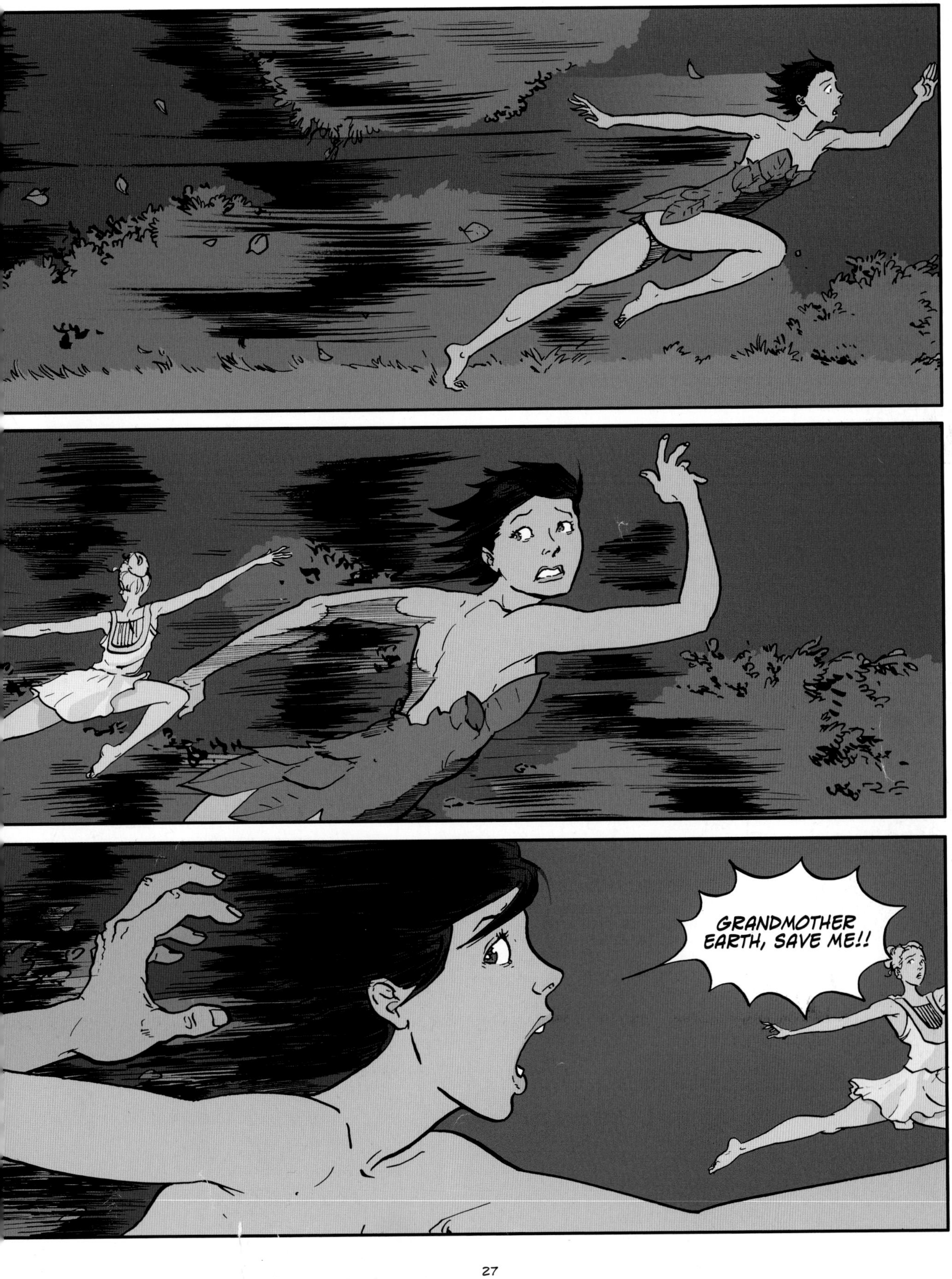
GRANDMOTHER EARTH, SAVE ME!!

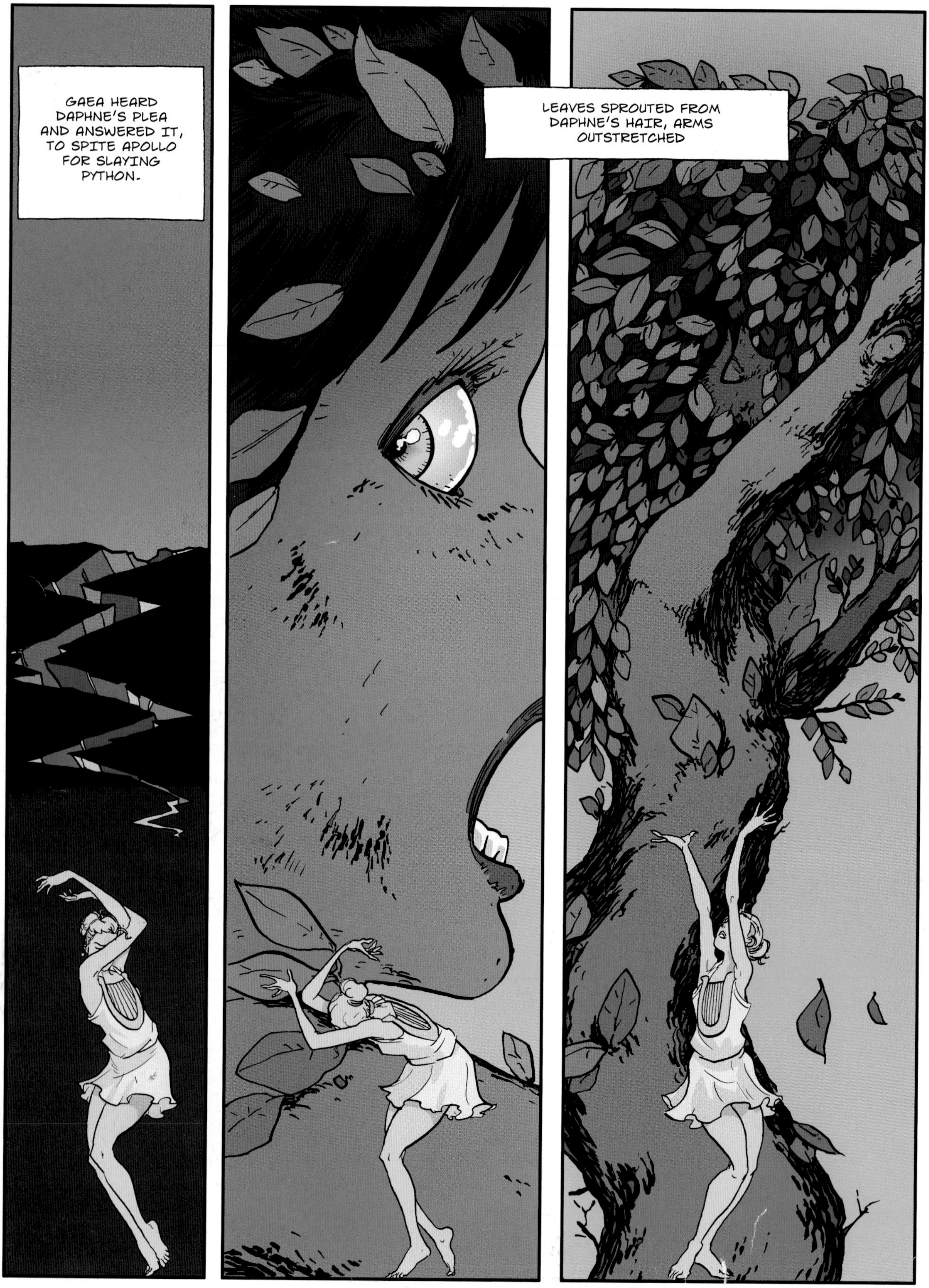
GAEA HEARD DAPHNE'S PLEA AND ANSWERED IT, TO SPITE APOLLO FOR SLAYING PYTHON.
LEAVES SPROUTED FROM DAPHNE'S HAIR, ARMS OUTSTRETCHED

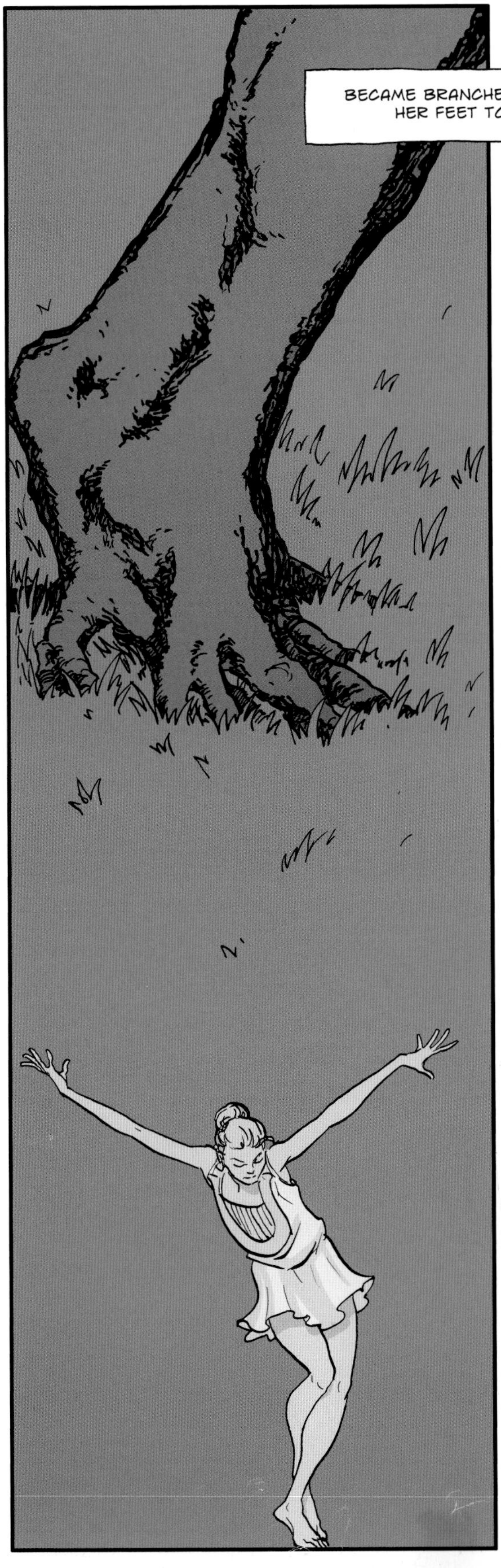

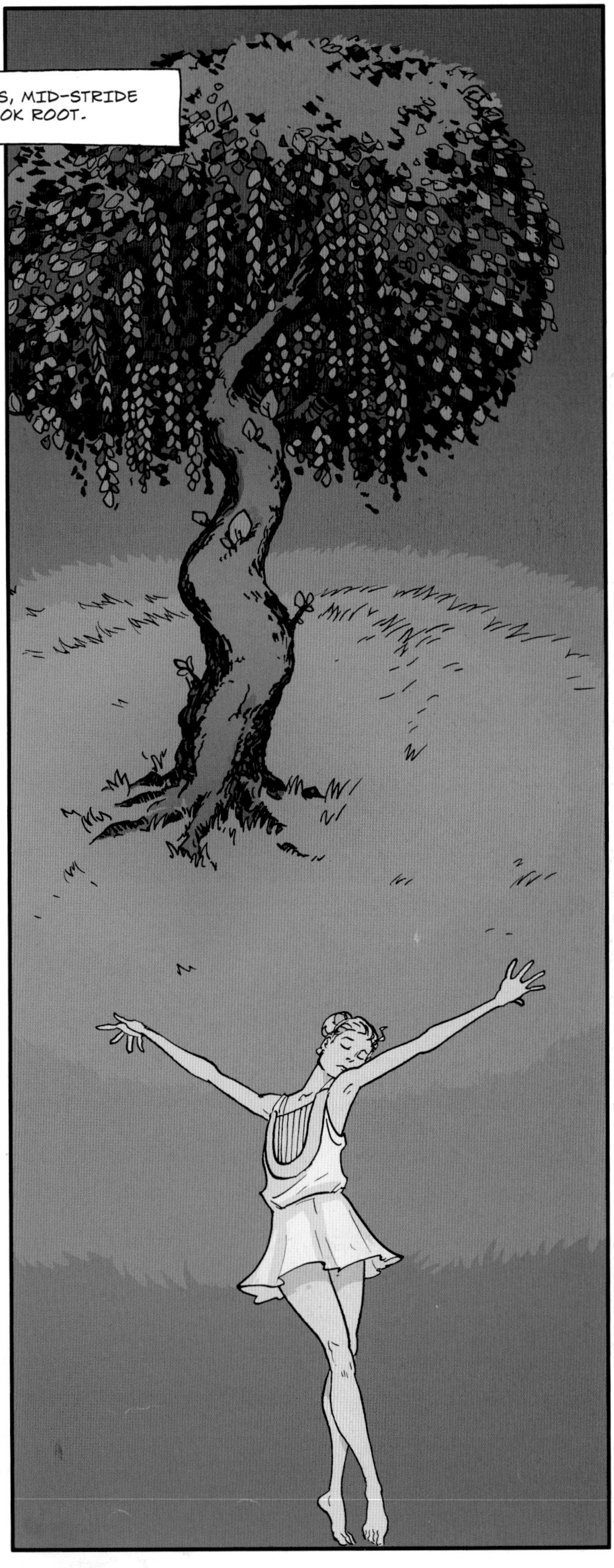
BECAME BRANCHES, MID-STRIDE HER FEET TOOK ROOT.

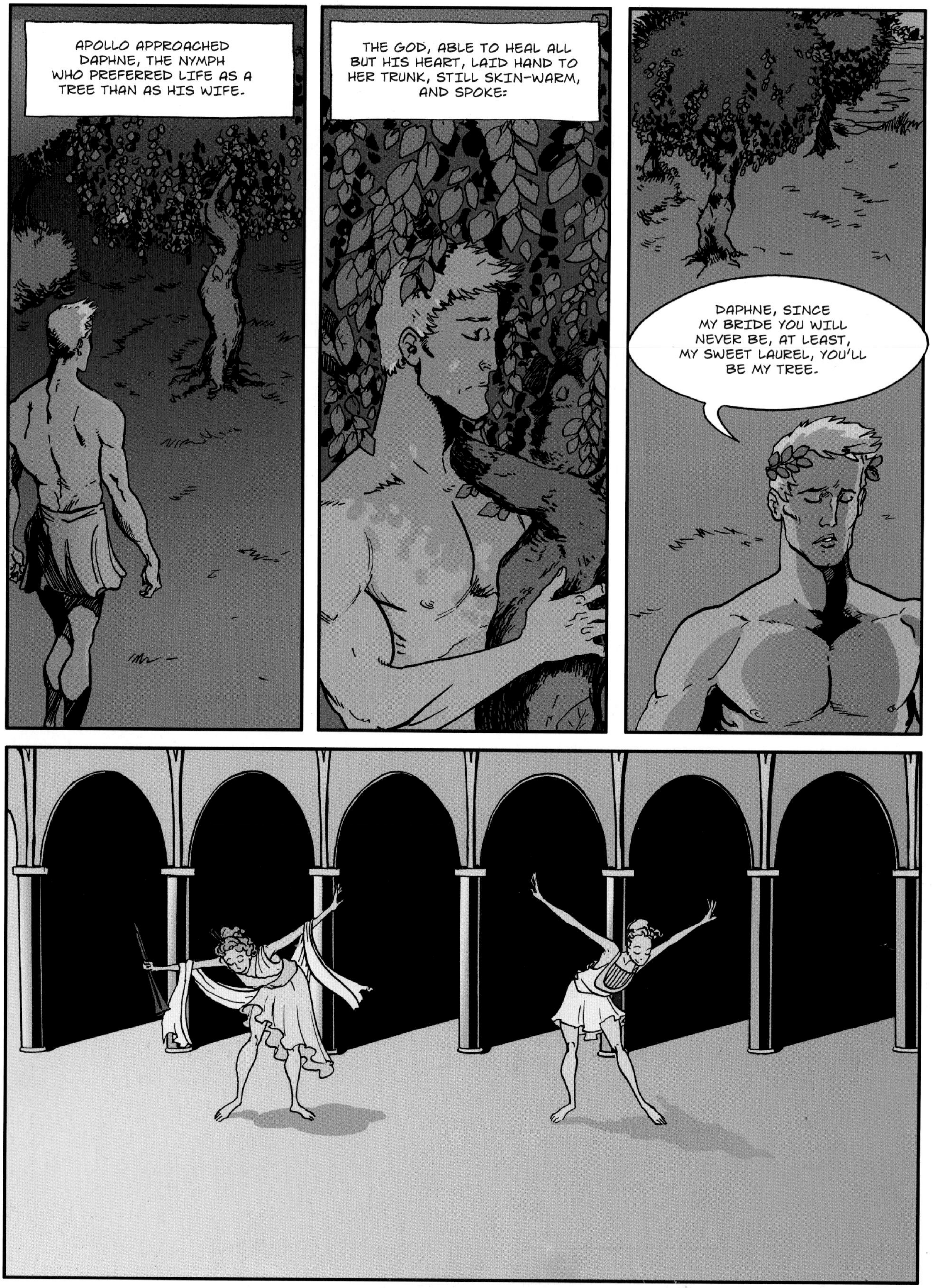
APOLLO APPROACHED DAPHNE, THE NYMPH WHO PREFERRED LIFE AS A TREE THAN AS HIS WIFE.
THE GOD, ABLE TO HEAL ALL BUT HIS HEART, LAID HAND TO HER TRUNK, STILL SKIN-WARM, AND SPOKE:
DAPHNE, SINCE MY BRIDE YOU WILL NEVER BE, AT LEAST, MY SWEET LAUREL, YOU'LL BE MY TREE.

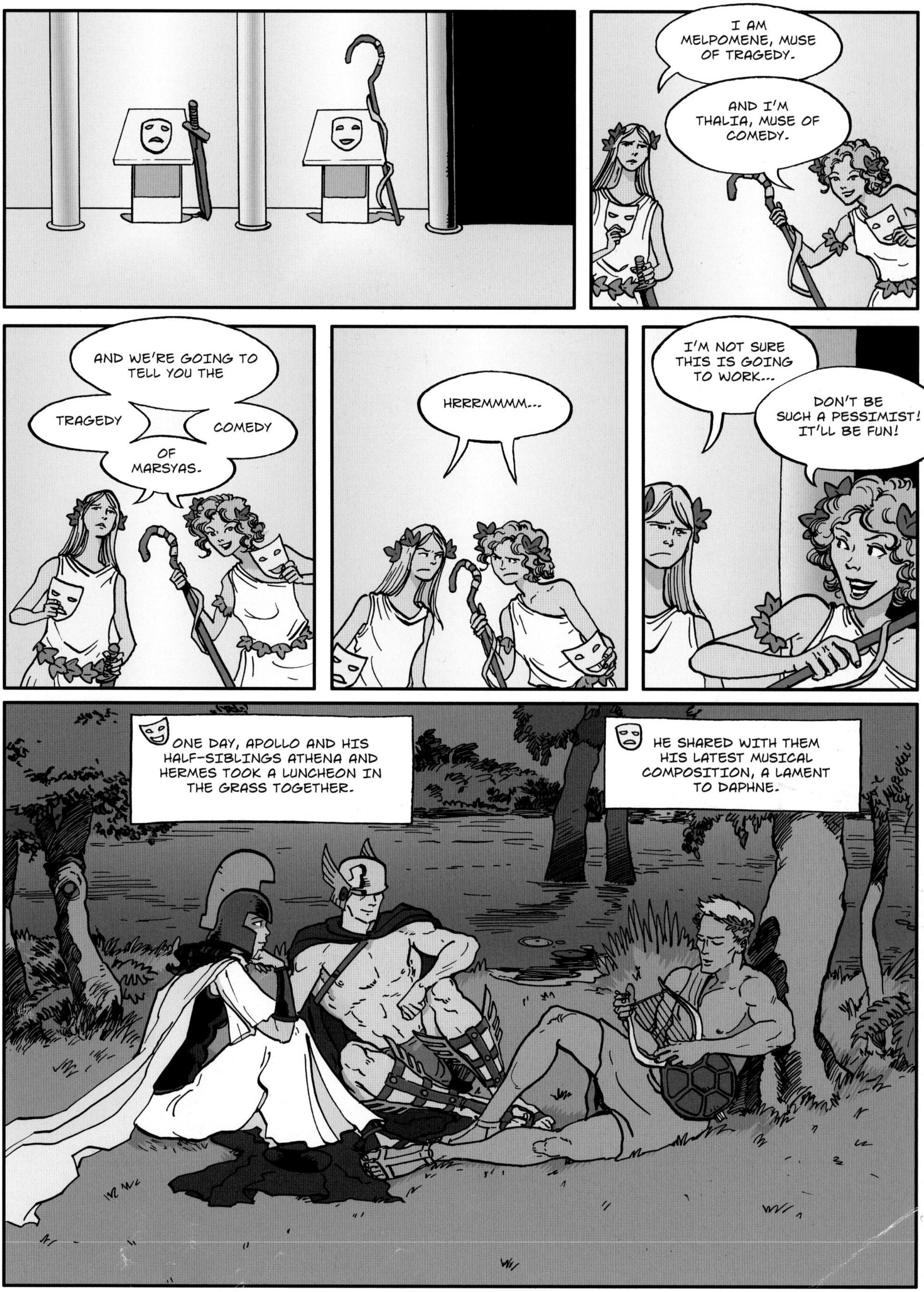

I AM MELPOMENE, MUSE OF TRAGEDY.
AND I'M THALIA, MUSE OF COMEDY.
AND WE'RE GOING TO TELL YOU THE
TRAGEDY
COMEDY
OF MARSYAS.
HRRRMMMM...
I'M NOT SURE THIS IS GOING TO WORK...
DON'T BE SUCH A PESSIMIST! IT'LL BE FUN!
ONE DAY, APOLLO AND HIS HALF-SIBLINGS ATHENA AND HERMES TOOK A LUNCHEON IN THE GRASS TOGETHER.
HE SHARED WITH THEM HIS LATEST MUSICAL COMPOSITION, A LAMENT TO DAPHNE.

—AND YOUR ETERNAL CROWN OF UNDYING LEAVES SHALL BE REFLECTED FOREVERMORE ON MY OWN EVER-YOUNG HEAD.

TRULY, APOLLO, YOUR SKILL ON THE LYRE IS WITHOUT COMPARE.

I INVENTED THAT, YOU KNOW.

HERMES, YOU INVENTED THE LYRE? CAN YOU PLAY AS WELL?

OH, SURE, I COULD PLAY IT EVEN BETTER, BUT I DON'T WANT TO MAKE APOLLO LOOK BAD.

NO YOU COULDN'T! I'M APOLLO! THERE'S NO ONE WHO PLAYS BETTER THAN ME! NO ONE!

OOOKAY...

IMPRESSED BY THE TALENTS OF HER HALF-BROTHERS, ATHENA ENDEAVORED TO CREATE A MUSICAL INVENTION OF HER OWN.

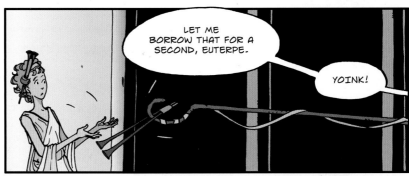
LET ME BORROW THAT FOR A SECOND, EUTERPE.

YOINK!

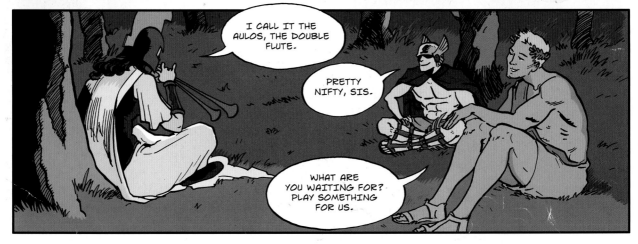
I CALL IT THE AULOS, THE DOUBLE FLUTE.

PRETTY NIFTY, SIS.

WHAT ARE YOU WAITING FOR? PLAY SOMETHING FOR US.

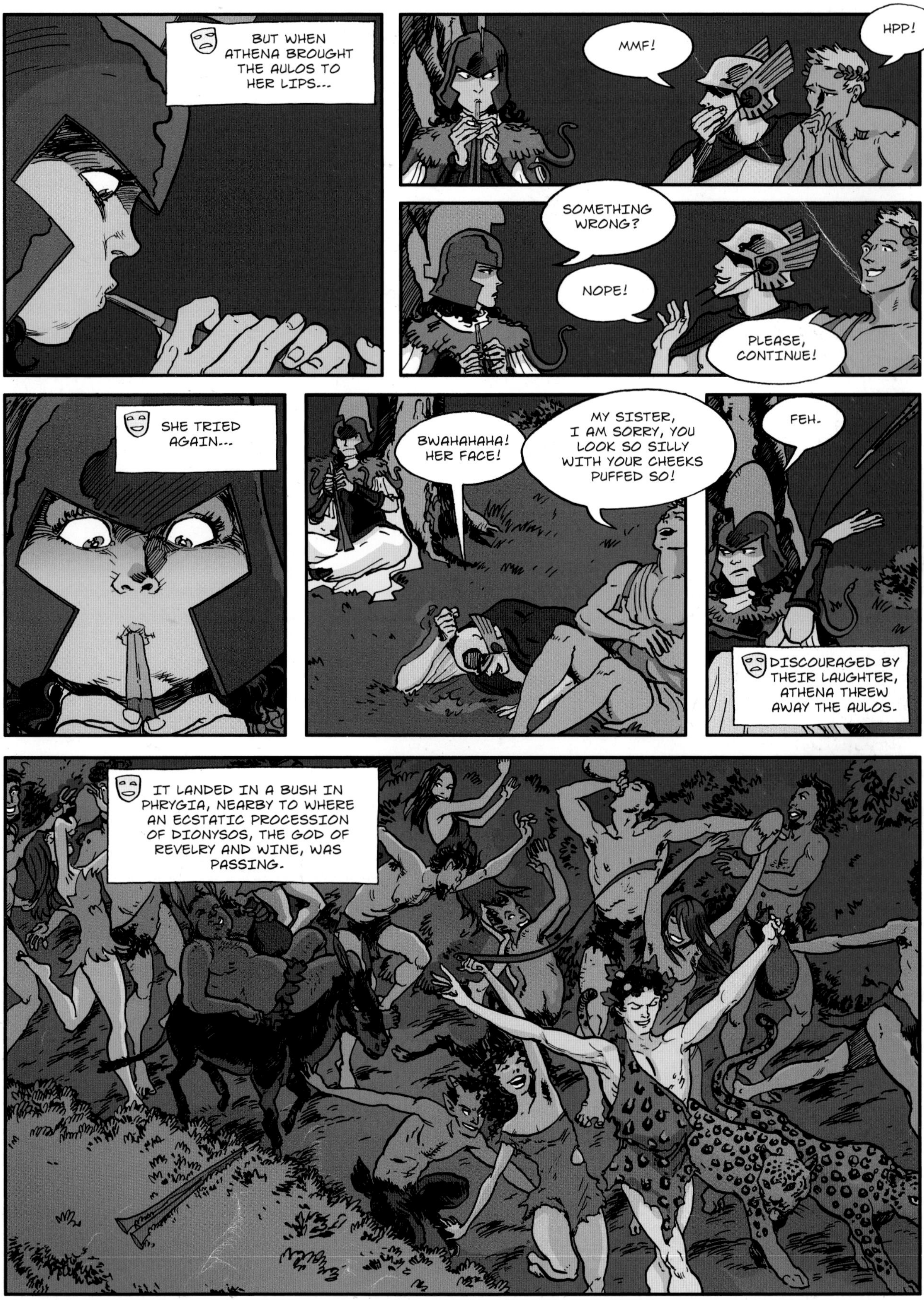
BUT WHEN ATHENA BROUGHT THE AULOS TO HER LIPS...
MMF!
HPP!
SOMETHING WRONG?
NOPE!
PLEASE, CONTINUE!
SHE TRIED AGAIN...
BWAHAHAHA! HER FACE!
MY SISTER, I AM SORRY, YOU LOOK SO SILLY WITH YOUR CHEEKS PUFFED SO!
FEH.
DISCOURAGED BY THEIR LAUGHTER, ATHENA THREW AWAY THE AULOS.
IT LANDED IN A BUSH IN PHRYGIA, NEARBY TO WHERE AN ECSTATIC PROCESSION OF DIONYSOS, THE GOD OF REVELRY AND WINE, WAS PASSING.

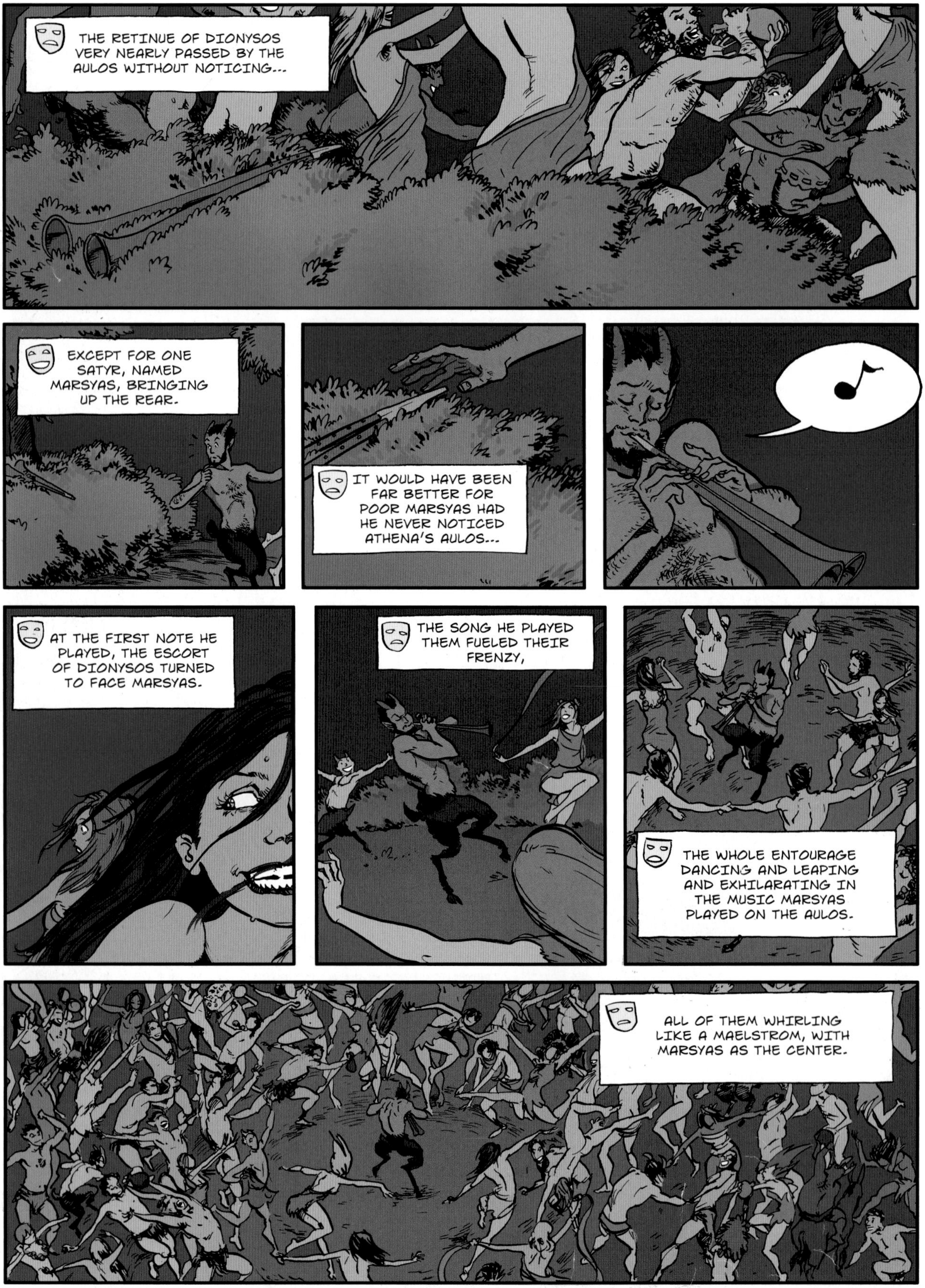
THE RETINUE OF DIONYSOS VERY NEARLY PASSED BY THE AULOS WITHOUT NOTICING...
EXCEPT FOR ONE SATYR, NAMED MARSYAS, BRINGING UP THE REAR.
IT WOULD HAVE BEEN FAR BETTER FOR POOR MARSYAS HAD HE NEVER NOTICED ATHENA'S AULOS...
♪
AT THE FIRST NOTE HE PLAYED, THE ESCORT OF DIONYSOS TURNED TO FACE MARSYAS.
THE SONG HE PLAYED THEM FUELED THEIR FRENZY,
THE WHOLE ENTOURAGE DANCING AND LEAPING AND EXHILARATING IN THE MUSIC MARSYAS PLAYED ON THE AULOS.
ALL OF THEM WHIRLING LIKE A MAELSTROM, WITH MARSYAS AS THE CENTER.

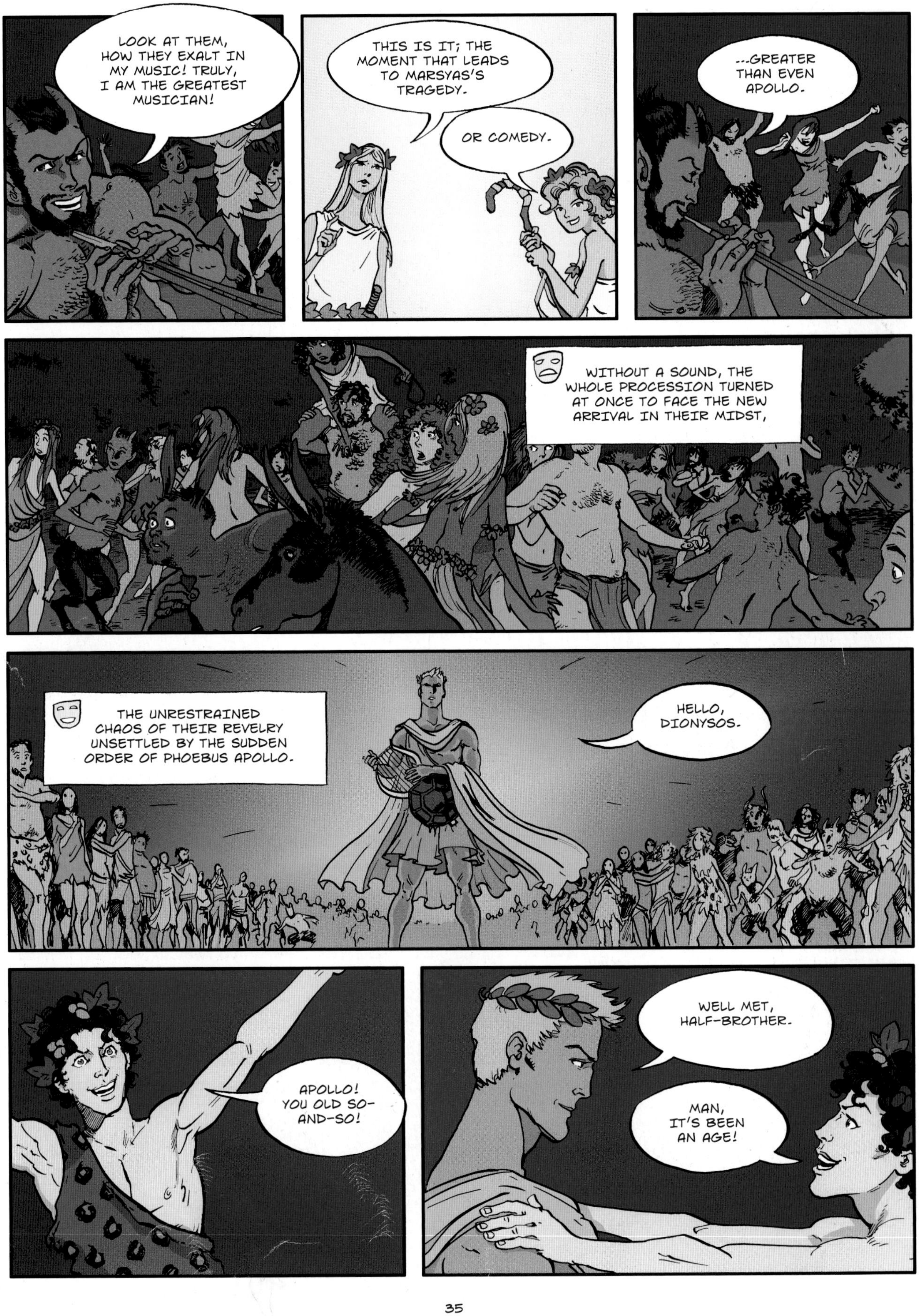

LOOK AT THEM, HOW THEY EXALT IN MY MUSIC! TRULY, I AM THE GREATEST MUSICIAN!
THIS IS IT; THE MOMENT THAT LEADS TO MARSYAS'S TRAGEDY.
OR COMEDY.
...GREATER THAN EVEN APOLLO.
WITHOUT A SOUND, THE WHOLE PROCESSION TURNED AT ONCE TO FACE THE NEW ARRIVAL IN THEIR MIDST,
THE UNRESTRAINED CHAOS OF THEIR REVELRY UNSETTLED BY THE SUDDEN ORDER OF PHOEBUS APOLLO.
HELLO, DIONYSOS.
APOLLO! YOU OLD SO-AND-SO!
WELL MET, HALF-BROTHER.
MAN, IT'S BEEN AN AGE!

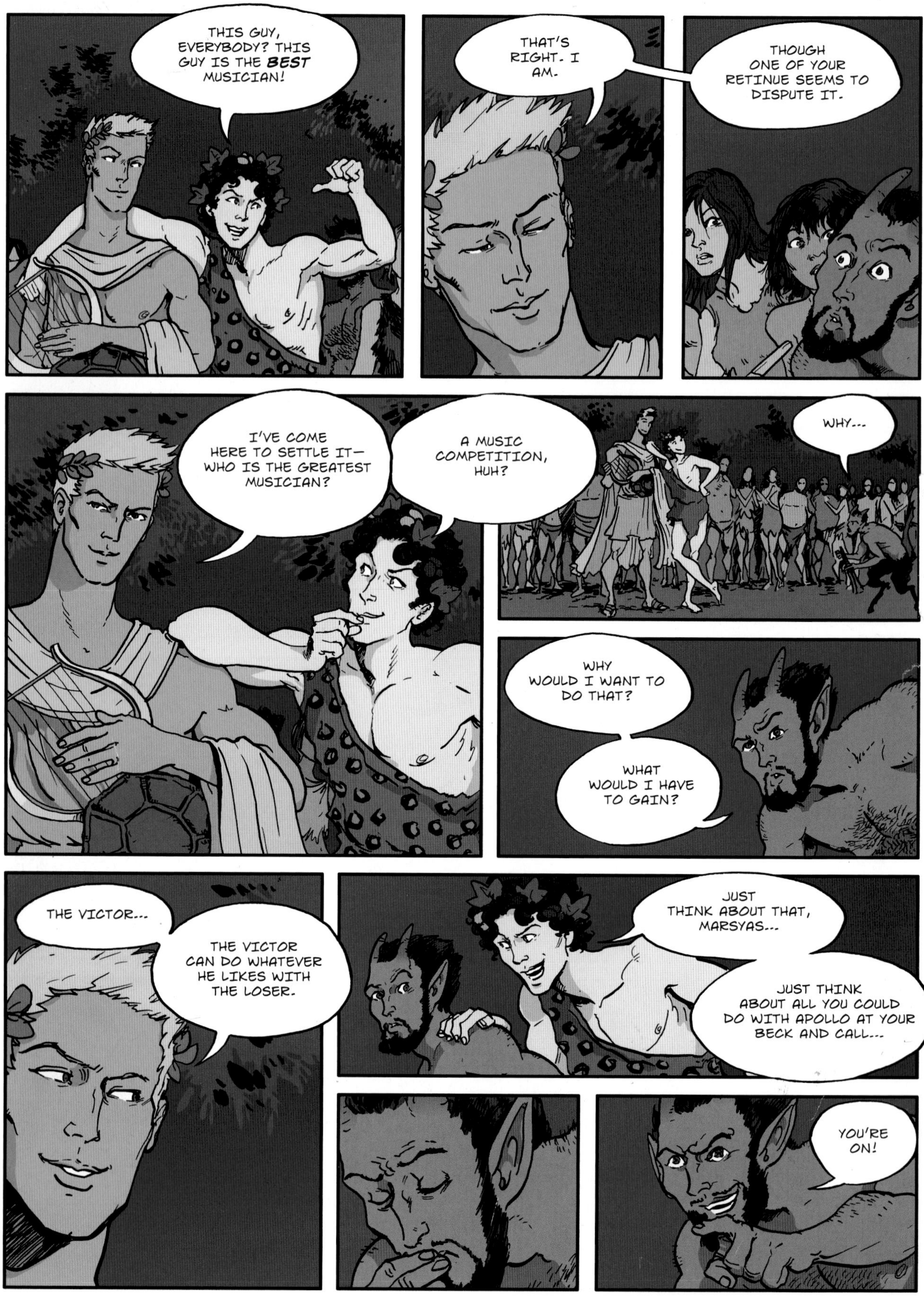
THIS GUY, EVERYBODY? THIS GUY IS THE **BEST** MUSICIAN!
THAT'S RIGHT. I AM.
THOUGH ONE OF YOUR RETINUE SEEMS TO DISPUTE IT.
I'VE COME HERE TO SETTLE IT— WHO IS THE GREATEST MUSICIAN?
A MUSIC COMPETITION, HUH?
WHY...
WHY WOULD I WANT TO DO THAT?
WHAT WOULD I HAVE TO GAIN?
THE VICTOR...
THE VICTOR CAN DO WHATEVER HE LIKES WITH THE LOSER.
JUST THINK ABOUT THAT, MARSYAS...
JUST THINK ABOUT ALL YOU COULD DO WITH APOLLO AT YOUR BECK AND CALL...
YOU'RE ON!

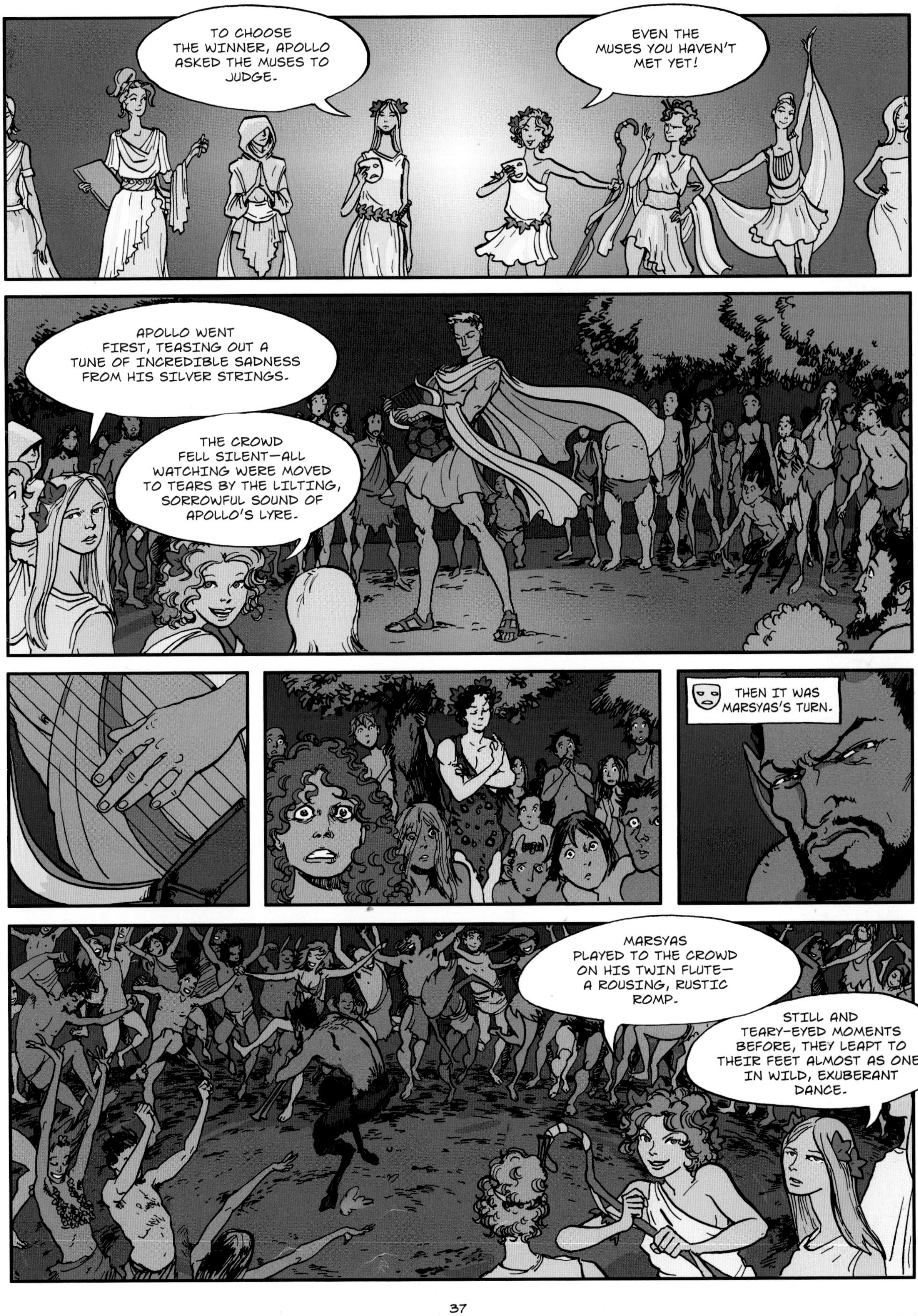

TO CHOOSE THE WINNER, APOLLO ASKED THE MUSES TO JUDGE.
EVEN THE MUSES YOU HAVEN'T MET YET!
APOLLO WENT FIRST, TEASING OUT A TUNE OF INCREDIBLE SADNESS FROM HIS SILVER STRINGS.
THE CROWD FELL SILENT—ALL WATCHING WERE MOVED TO TEARS BY THE LILTING, SORROWFUL SOUND OF APOLLO'S LYRE.
THEN IT WAS MARSYAS'S TURN.
MARSYAS PLAYED TO THE CROWD ON HIS TWIN FLUTE—A ROUSING, RUSTIC ROMP.
STILL AND TEARY-EYED MOMENTS BEFORE, THEY LEAPT TO THEIR FEET ALMOST AS ONE, IN WILD, EXUBERANT DANCE.

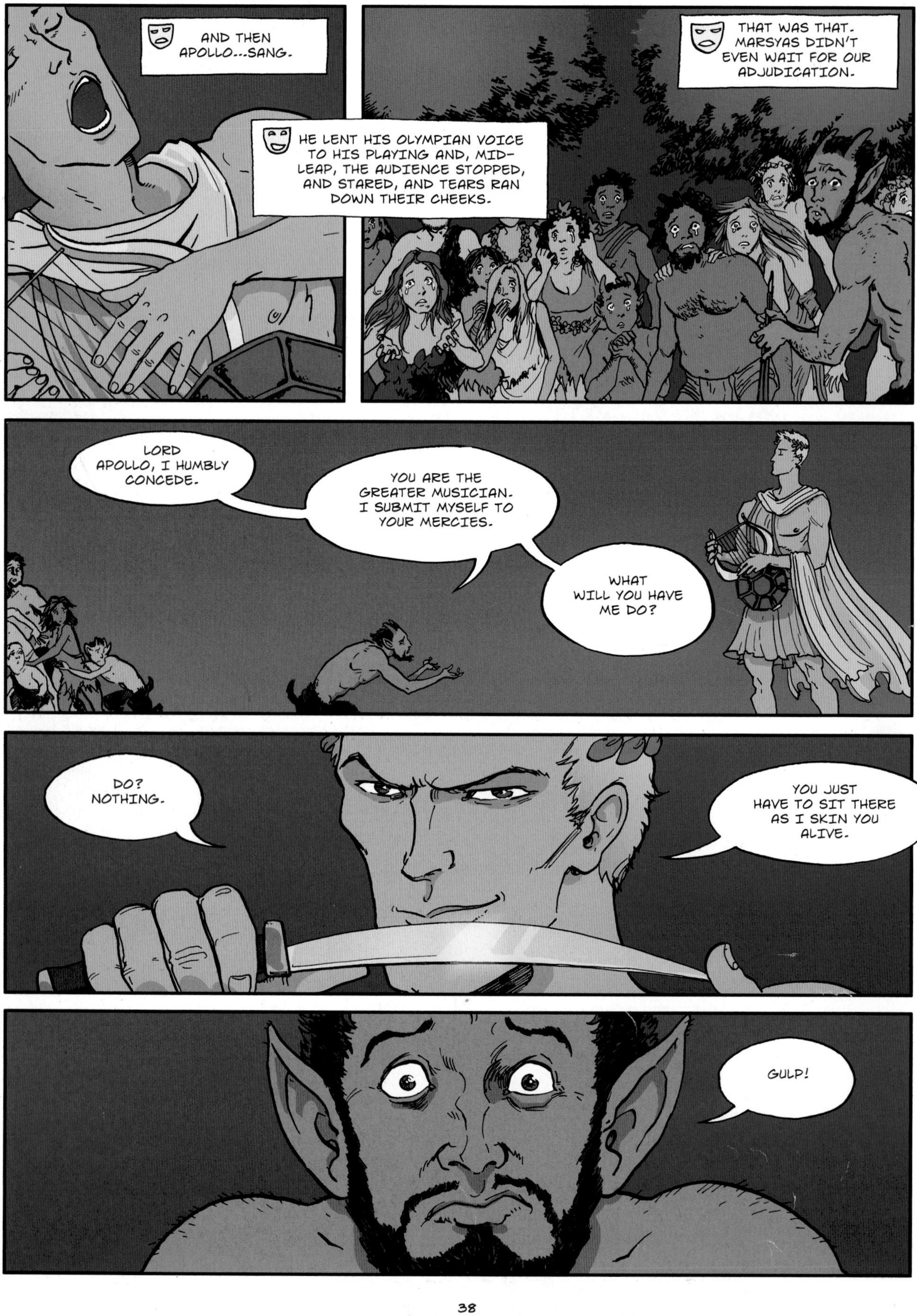
AND THEN APOLLO...SANG.
HE LENT HIS OLYMPIAN VOICE TO HIS PLAYING AND, MID-LEAP, THE AUDIENCE STOPPED, AND STARED, AND TEARS RAN DOWN THEIR CHEEKS.
THAT WAS THAT. MARSYAS DIDN'T EVEN WAIT FOR OUR ADJUDICATION.
LORD APOLLO, I HUMBLY CONCEDE.
YOU ARE THE GREATER MUSICIAN. I SUBMIT MYSELF TO YOUR MERCIES.
WHAT WILL YOU HAVE ME DO?
DO? NOTHING.
YOU JUST HAVE TO SIT THERE AS I SKIN YOU ALIVE.
GULP!

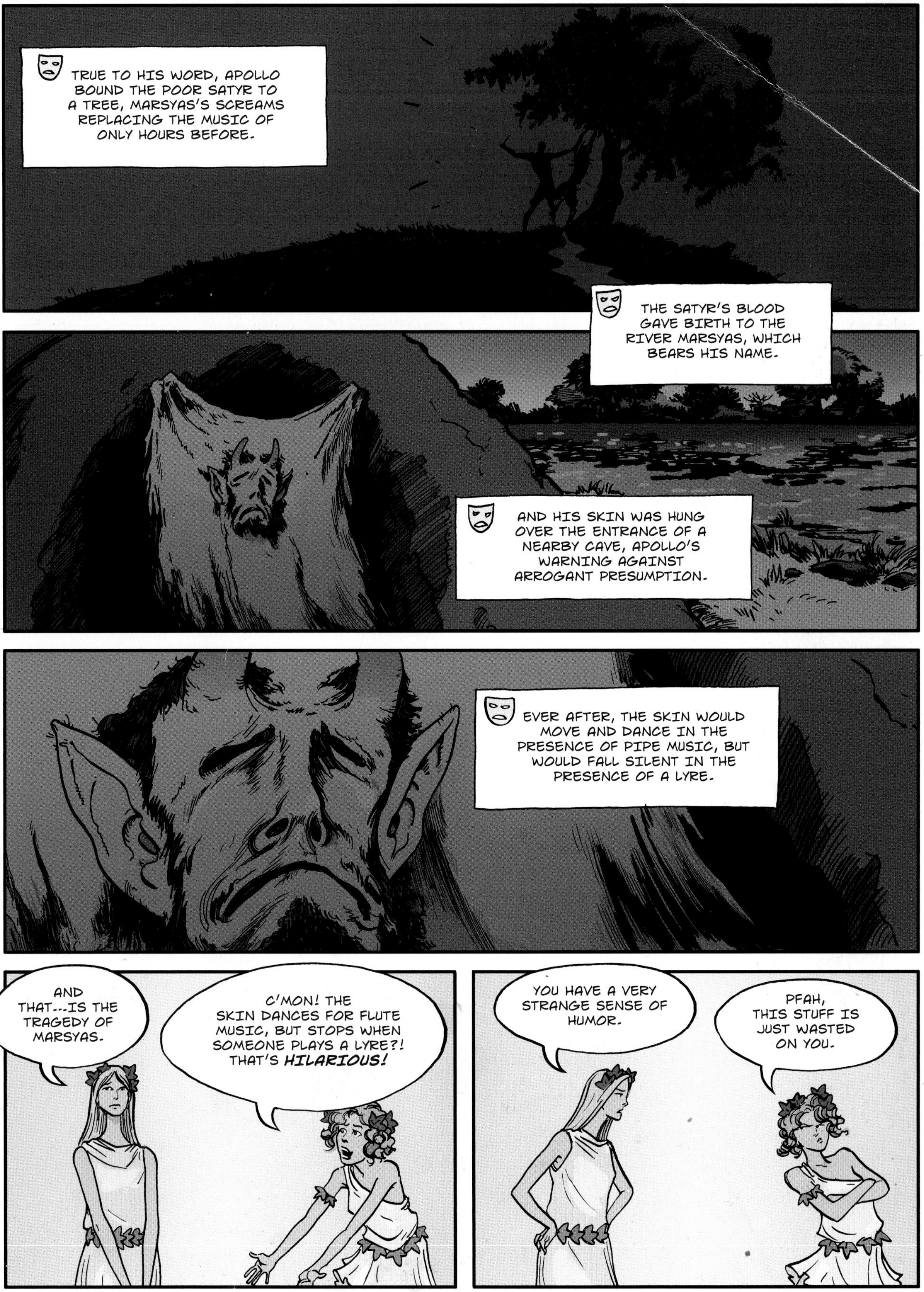
TRUE TO HIS WORD, APOLLO BOUND THE POOR SATYR TO A TREE, MARSYAS'S SCREAMS REPLACING THE MUSIC OF ONLY HOURS BEFORE.
THE SATYR'S BLOOD GAVE BIRTH TO THE RIVER MARSYAS, WHICH BEARS HIS NAME.
AND HIS SKIN WAS HUNG OVER THE ENTRANCE OF A NEARBY CAVE, APOLLO'S WARNING AGAINST ARROGANT PRESUMPTION.
EVER AFTER, THE SKIN WOULD MOVE AND DANCE IN THE PRESENCE OF PIPE MUSIC, BUT WOULD FALL SILENT IN THE PRESENCE OF A LYRE.
AND THAT---IS THE TRAGEDY OF MARSYAS.
C'MON! THE SKIN DANCES FOR FLUTE MUSIC, BUT STOPS WHEN SOMEONE PLAYS A LYRE?! THAT'S ***HILARIOUS!***
YOU HAVE A VERY STRANGE SENSE OF HUMOR.
PFAH, THIS STUFF IS JUST WASTED ON YOU.

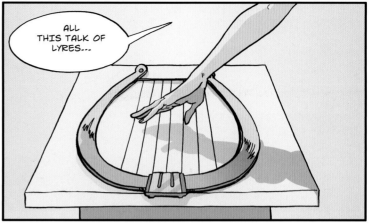

ALL THIS TALK OF LYRES...

GREETINGS, LISTENERS. I AM ERATO, THE MUSE OF BOTH MIMICRY AND LOVE POETRY.

I'LL RECITE YOU NOW A POEM OF LOVE OF APOLLO, WHO HAS HAD MANY LOVES.

WHY, ALL NINE OF WE MUSES COUNT AMONG THAT NUMBER. BUT THIS STORY IS NOT ABOUT US...

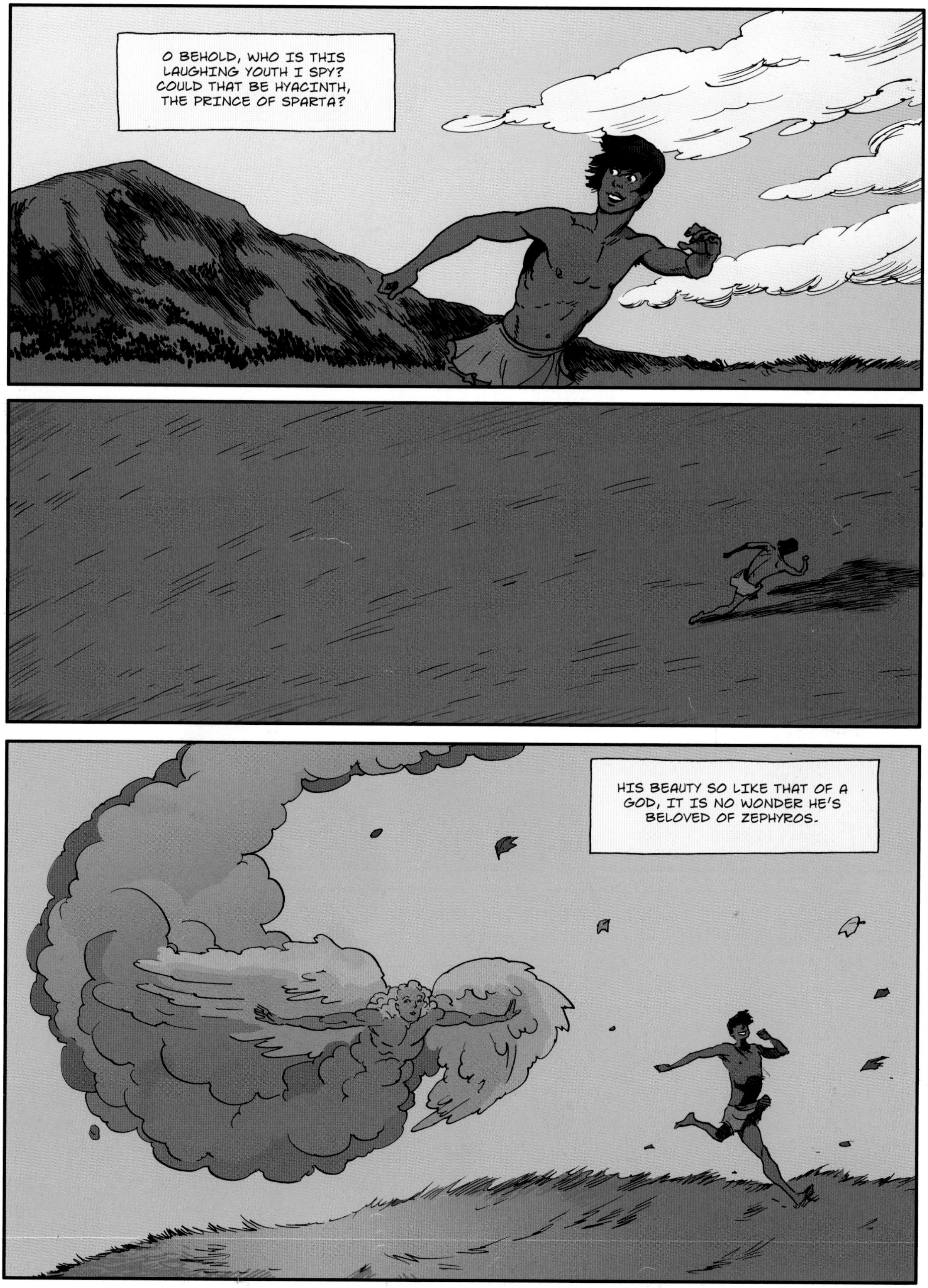
O BEHOLD, WHO IS THIS LAUGHING YOUTH I SPY? COULD THAT BE HYACINTH, THE PRINCE OF SPARTA?
HIS BEAUTY SO LIKE THAT OF A GOD, IT IS NO WONDER HE'S BELOVED OF ZEPHYROS.

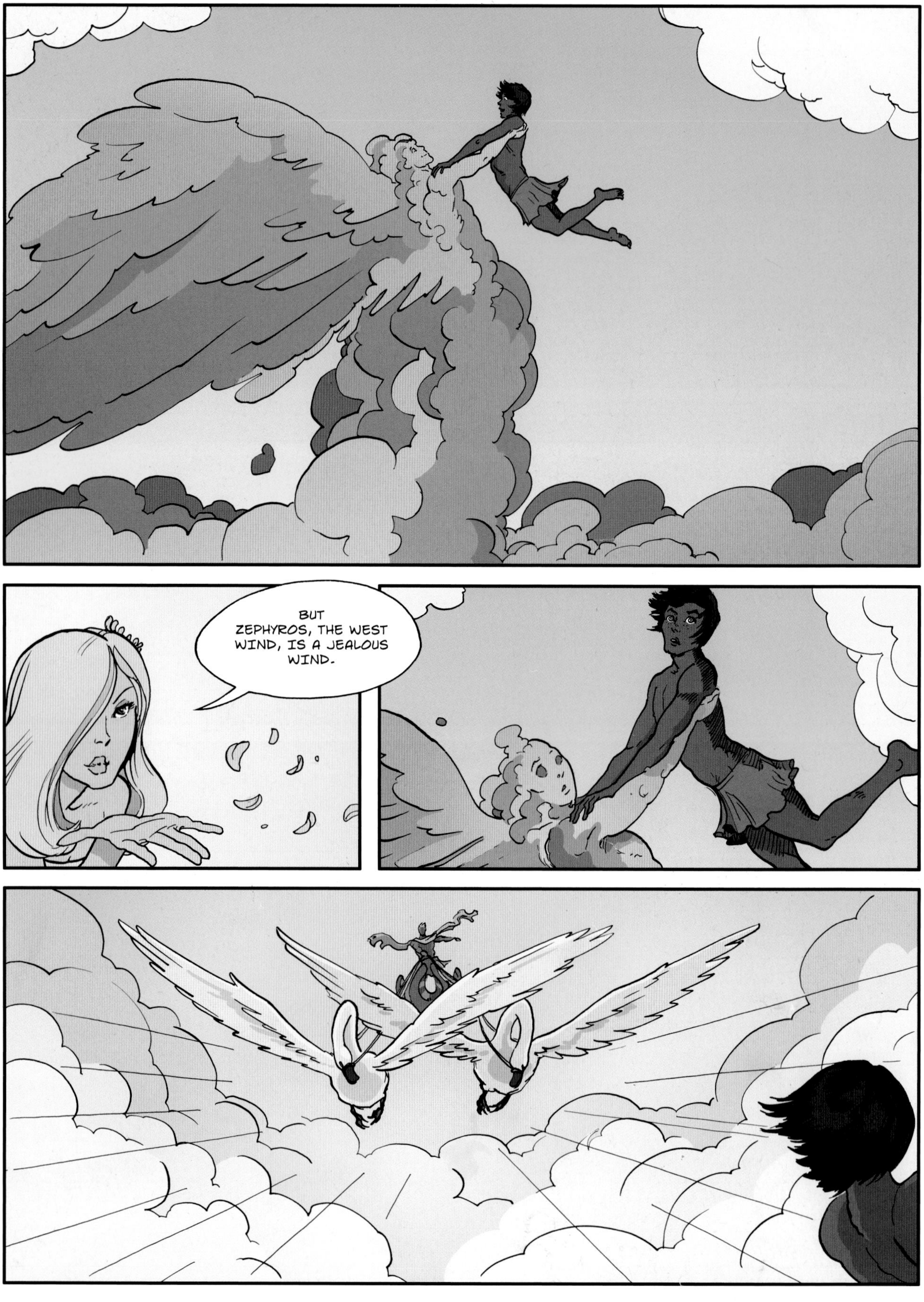
BUT ZEPHYROS, THE WEST WIND, IS A JEALOUS WIND.

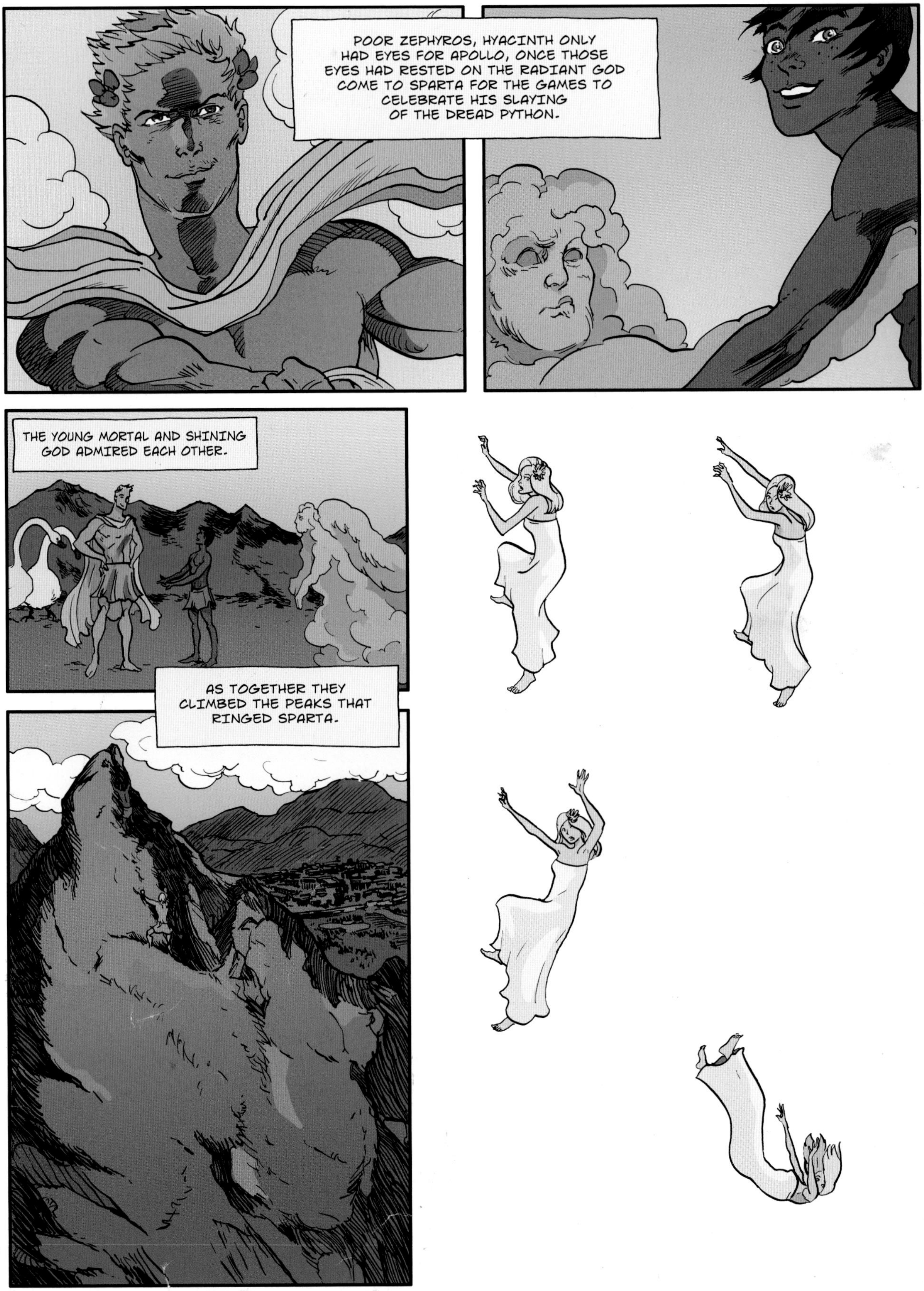
POOR ZEPHYROS, HYACINTH ONLY HAD EYES FOR APOLLO, ONCE THOSE EYES HAD RESTED ON THE RADIANT GOD COME TO SPARTA FOR THE GAMES TO CELEBRATE HIS SLAYING OF THE DREAD PYTHON.
THE YOUNG MORTAL AND SHINING GOD ADMIRED EACH OTHER.
AS TOGETHER THEY CLIMBED THE PEAKS THAT RINGED SPARTA.

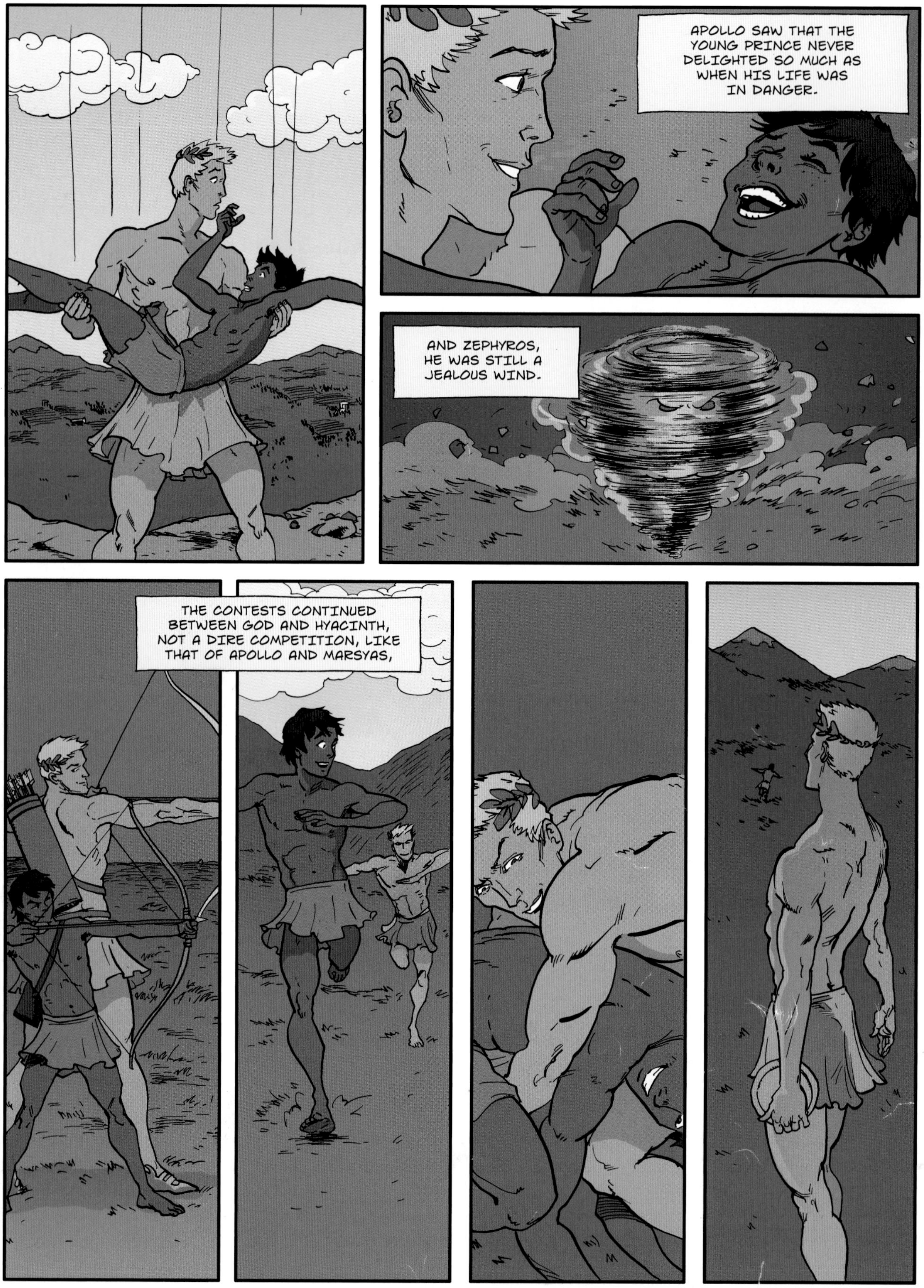
APOLLO SAW THAT THE YOUNG PRINCE NEVER DELIGHTED SO MUCH AS WHEN HIS LIFE WAS IN DANGER.
AND ZEPHYROS, HE WAS STILL A JEALOUS WIND.
THE CONTESTS CONTINUED BETWEEN GOD AND HYACINTH, NOT A DIRE COMPETITION, LIKE THAT OF APOLLO AND MARSYAS,

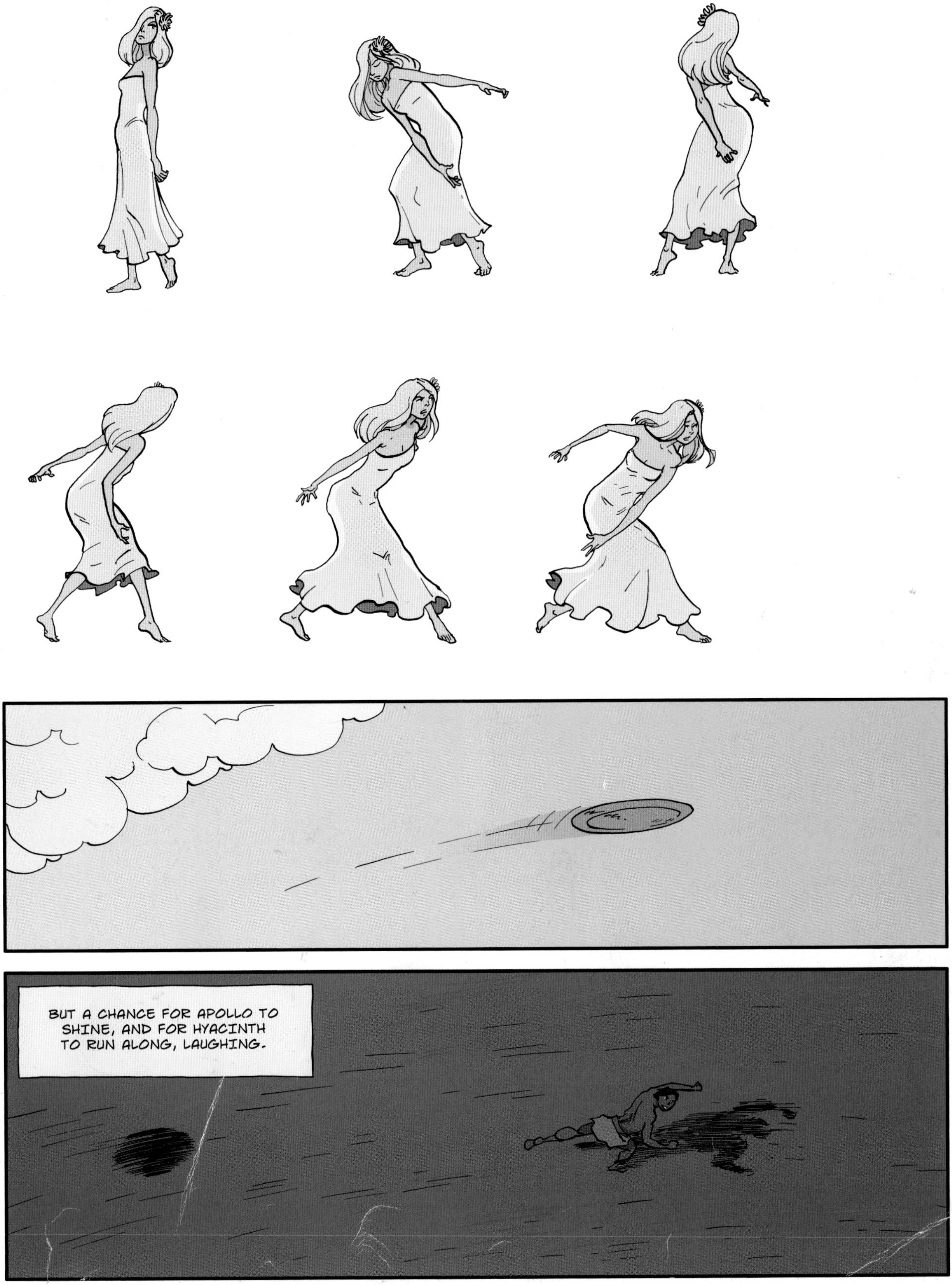
BUT A CHANCE FOR APOLLO TO SHINE, AND FOR HYACINTH TO RUN ALONG, LAUGHING.

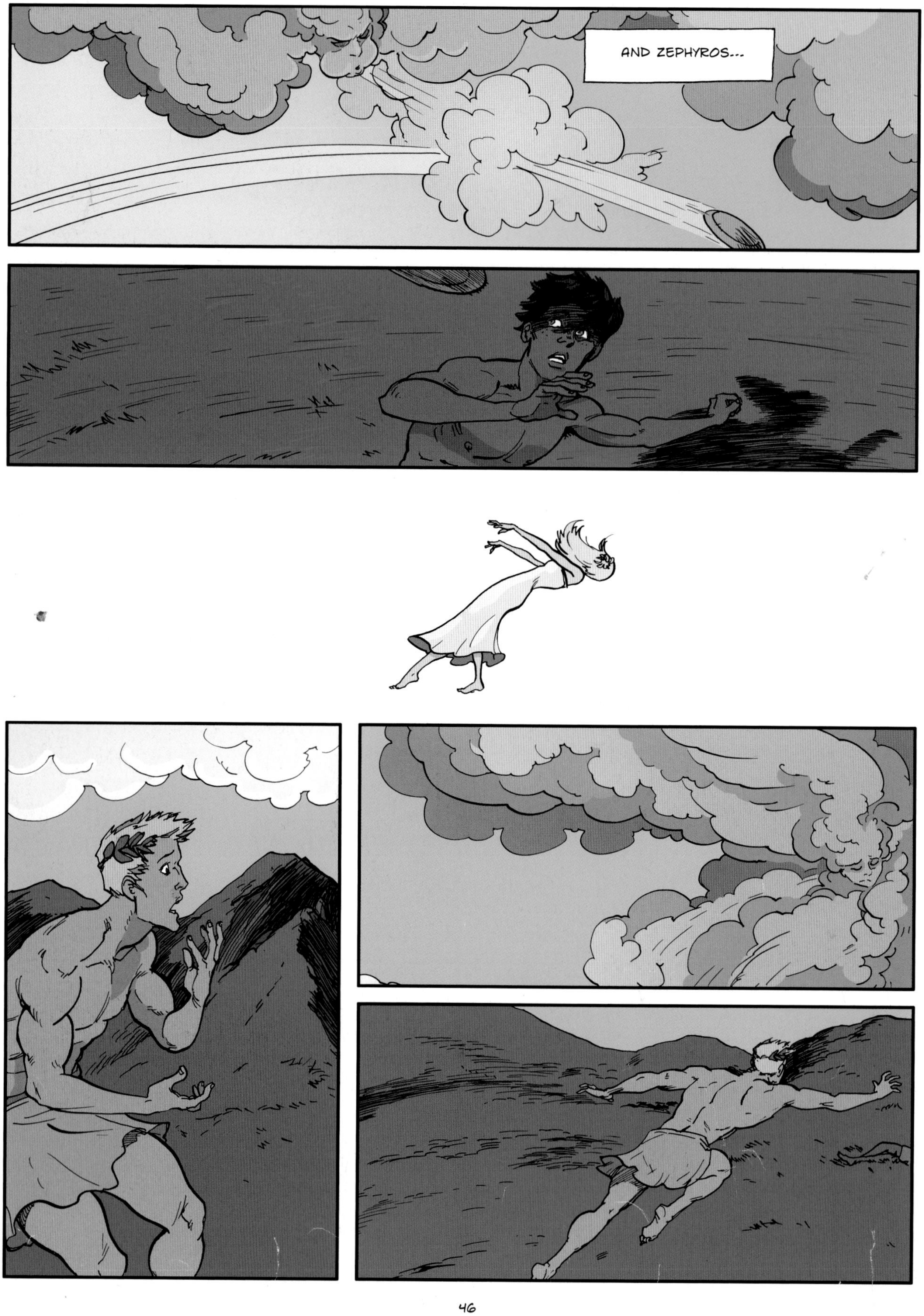
AND ZEPHYROS...

STRICKEN BY THE ERRANT DISCUS, HYACINTH WAS BEYOND THE SKILLS OF EVEN HEALER APOLLO TO RESCUE, THOUGH TRY HE DID ADMINISTERING NECTAR AND AMBROSIA, FOOD OF THE GODS.

BUT IT WAS TOO LATE.

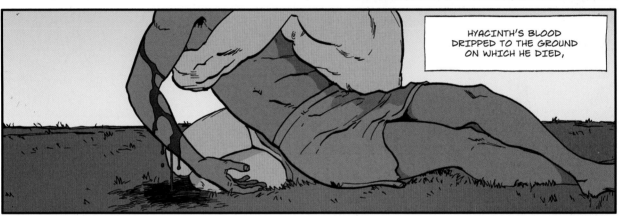

HYACINTH'S BLOOD DRIPPED TO THE GROUND ON WHICH HE DIED,

TRANSFORMED TO THE FLOWER WHICH BEARS HIS NAME,

APOLLO'S TRIBUTE TO THE MORTAL PRINCE HE LOVED AND LOST TO ZEPHYROS, THE JEALOUS WIND.

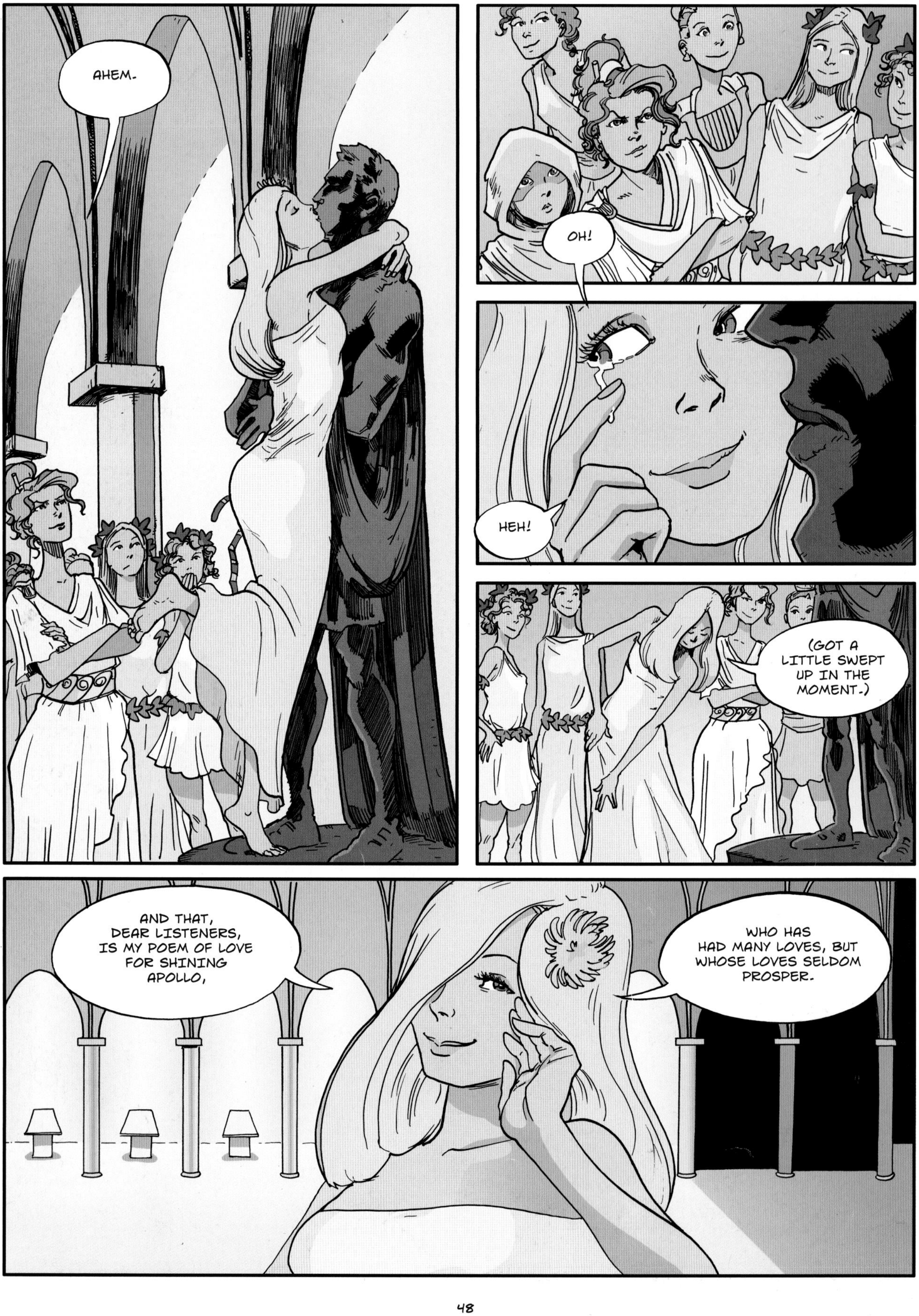
AHEM.
OH!
HEH!
(GOT A LITTLE SWEPT UP IN THE MOMENT.)
AND THAT, DEAR LISTENERS, IS MY POEM OF LOVE FOR SHINING APOLLO,
WHO HAS HAD MANY LOVES, BUT WHOSE LOVES SELDOM PROSPER.

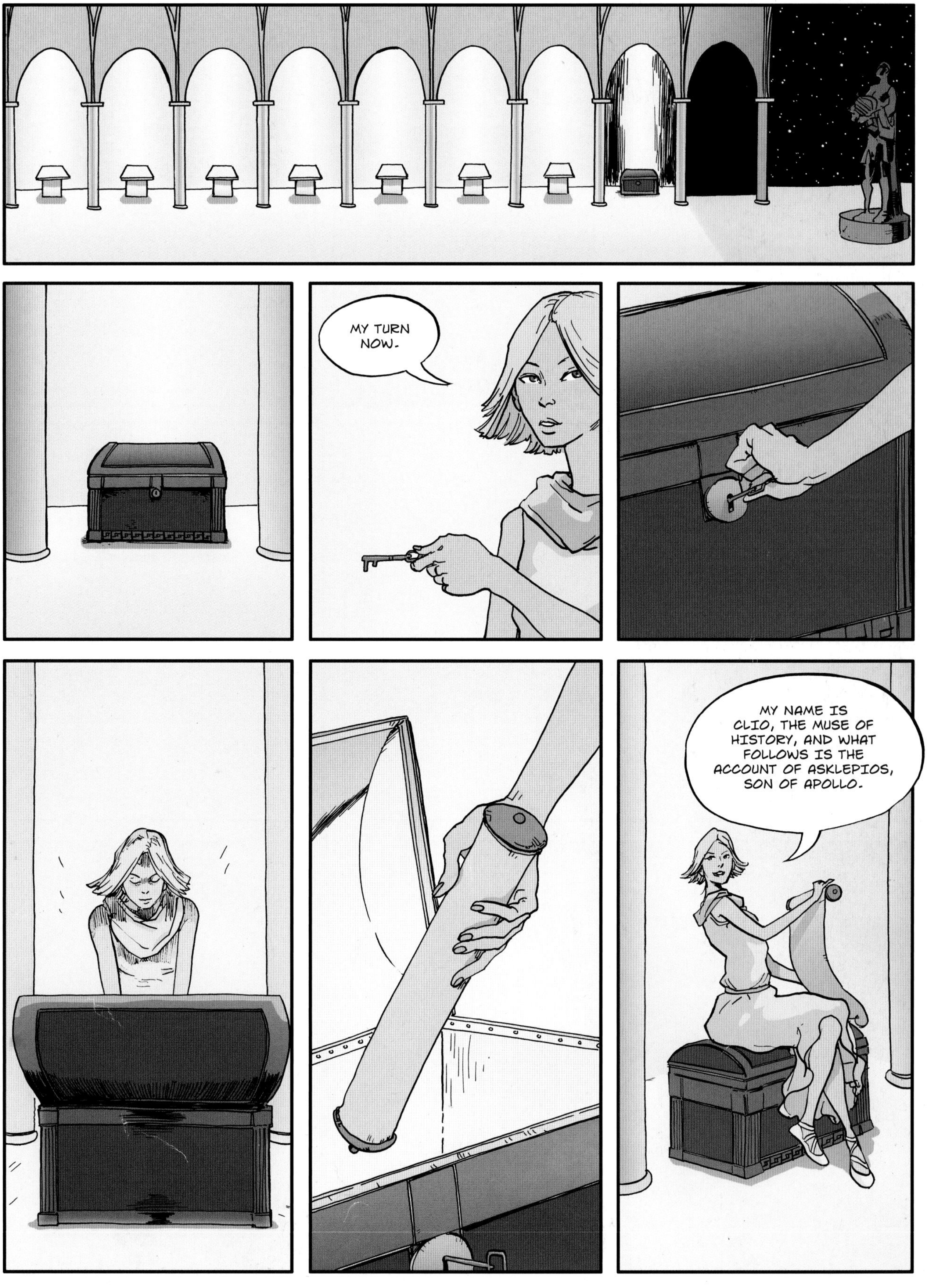
MY TURN NOW.
MY NAME IS CLIO, THE MUSE OF HISTORY, AND WHAT FOLLOWS IS THE ACCOUNT OF ASKLEPIOS, SON OF APOLLO.

AS HE WAS WONT TO DO, APOLLO FELL IN LOVE WITH A MORTAL WOMAN, A THESSALIAN PRINCESS NAMED KORONIS.

APOLLO WAS AWAY MUCH OF THE TIME, AND HE SET A WHITE CROW TO KEEP WATCH OVER KORONIS.

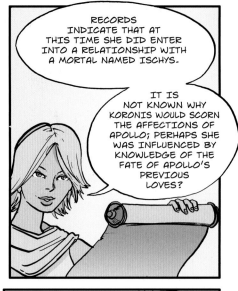

RECORDS INDICATE THAT AT THIS TIME SHE DID ENTER INTO A RELATIONSHIP WITH A MORTAL NAMED ISCHYS.

IT IS NOT KNOWN WHY KORONIS WOULD SCORN THE AFFECTIONS OF APOLLO; PERHAPS SHE WAS INFLUENCED BY KNOWLEDGE OF THE FATE OF APOLLO'S PREVIOUS LOVES?

APOLLO WAS ENRAGED WHEN HE LEARNED OF KORONIS'S INFIDELITY.

HE ERUPTED, HIS RADIANCE SCORCHING THE VERY AIR AROUND HIM.

HISTORICAL NOTE: THIS IS WHY ALL CROWS ARE NOW BLACK.

HE ENLISTED HIS SISTER, ARTEMIS, TO DO THE DEED.

HE HAD NOT THE HEART TO DO IT HIMSELF, AND HIS SISTER'S ARROWS KILLED WITHOUT PAIN.

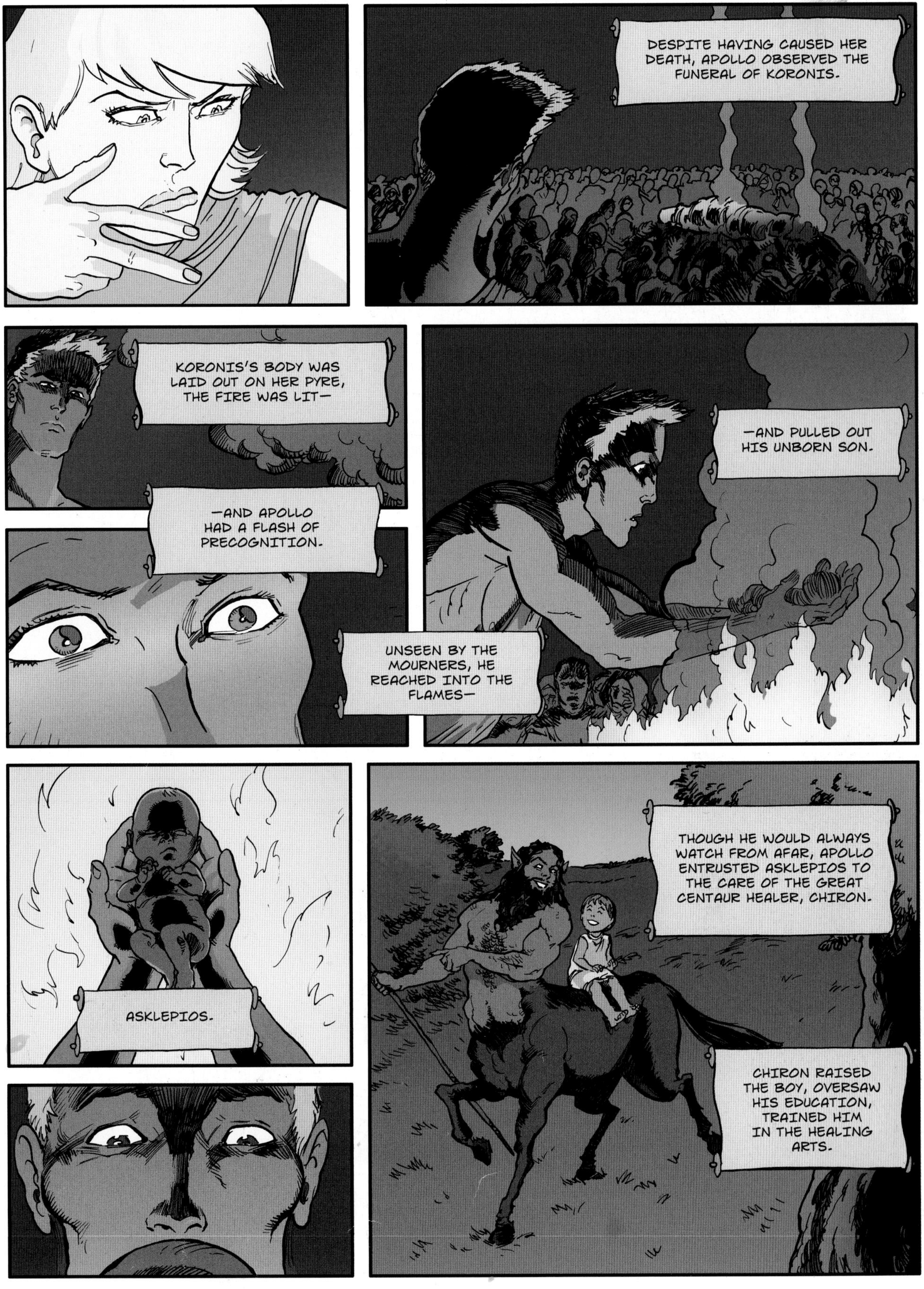
DESPITE HAVING CAUSED HER DEATH, APOLLO OBSERVED THE FUNERAL OF KORONIS.
KORONIS'S BODY WAS LAID OUT ON HER PYRE, THE FIRE WAS LIT—
—AND APOLLO HAD A FLASH OF PRECOGNITION.
UNSEEN BY THE MOURNERS, HE REACHED INTO THE FLAMES—
—AND PULLED OUT HIS UNBORN SON.
ASKLEPIOS.
THOUGH HE WOULD ALWAYS WATCH FROM AFAR, APOLLO ENTRUSTED ASKLEPIOS TO THE CARE OF THE GREAT CENTAUR HEALER, CHIRON.
CHIRON RAISED THE BOY, OVERSAW HIS EDUCATION, TRAINED HIM IN THE HEALING ARTS.

ASKLEPIOS WAS THE GREATEST STUDENT I EVER HAD.

HE HAD ALL HIS FATHER'S INNATE HEALING SKILLS, PLUS ALL OF MY TEACHINGS.

AND AN UNCANNY SENSE OF WONDER FOR THE WORLD ABOUT HIM.

HE OBSERVED EVERYTHING, CONSTANTLY.

HE SAW THE HIDDEN RITUALS OF THE SNAKES. HE LEARNED THEIR SECRETS.

ASKLEPIOS KNEW THINGS EVEN I DO NOT KNOW.

HE KNEW THINGS EVEN HIS *FATHER* DID NOT KNOW.

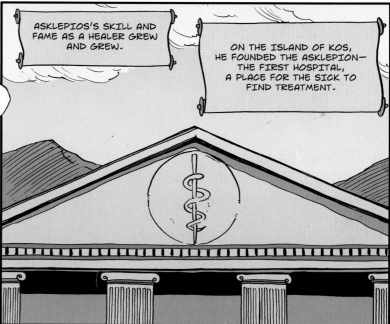

ASKLEPIOS'S SKILL AND FAME AS A HEALER GREW AND GREW.

ON THE ISLAND OF KOS, HE FOUNDED THE ASKLEPION— THE FIRST HOSPITAL, A PLACE FOR THE SICK TO FIND TREATMENT.

ASKLEPIOS AND HIS DAUGHTERS, HYGEIA AND PANACEA, TENDED TO THEIR PATIENTS. UNTOLD NUMBERS OF MORTALS HAD THEIR LIVES ENRICHED AND EXTENDED BY ASKLEPIOS AND THE TECHNIQUES HE PIONEERED.

HE TRAINED A SMALL ARMY OF ASKLEPIADAE—THE FIRST DOCTORS.

THE ASKLEPIADAE WENT FORTH AND FOUNDED MORE ASKLEPIONS, MORE HOSPITALS.

LIFE EVERYWHERE WAS GETTING BETTER, BECAUSE OF ASKLEPIOS.

APOLLO OBSERVED THIS ALL AND BEAMED WITH PRIDE.

MANY WHO KNEW HIM WERE SURPRISED BY THIS CHANGE.

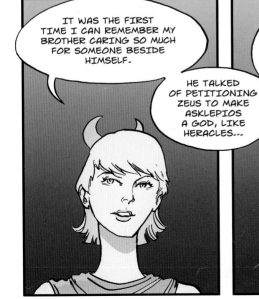

IT WAS THE FIRST TIME I CAN REMEMBER MY BROTHER CARING SO MUCH FOR SOMEONE BESIDE HIMSELF.

HE TALKED OF PETITIONING ZEUS TO MAKE ASKLEPIOS A GOD, LIKE HERACLES...

I REMEMBER HADES BEING ANNOYED THAT ASKLEPIOS WAS SAVING SO MANY MORTALS. IT'S POINTLESS, HE'D SAY, HE'S JUST CREATING A GLITCH IN THE SYSTEM.

SOONER OR LATER, THEY'LL ALL BE MY GUESTS.

ONE DAY, ASKLEPIOS WAS SUMMONED TO ATHENS.

HE FOUND HIMSELF IN AUDIENCE WITH THESEUS, KING OF ATHENS. THE EXACT TRANSCRIPT OF THEIR MEETING WAS NOT RECORDED, BUT WHAT IS KNOWN IS THIS:

ΘΗΣΕΥΣ   ΑΙΓΕΥΣ   ΠΑΝΔΙΩΝ

PRINCE HIPPOLYTUS LAY INJURED AND NEAR DEATH.

ASKLEPIOS WAS TOLD, IN NO UNCERTAIN TERMS, TO SAVE HIM, OR ELSE.

ASKLEPIOS LOOKED IN ON THE PRINCE.

HE HAD JUST DIED. HIS SHADE HAD DEPARTED.

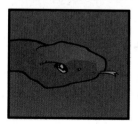

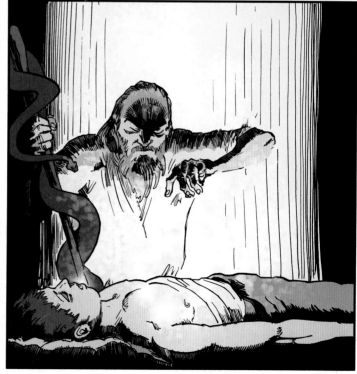

HUH
BUH WHA?

IT WAS THE DARNDEST THING.

ONE SECOND, I'M RACING ALONG, ESCORTING THE SHADE OF HIPPOLYTUS TO THE UNDERWORLD—THE NEXT SECOND, HE DISAPPEARS OUT OF MY HAND!

BACK TO EARTH, BECAUSE HE'S BREATHING AGAIN! NOTHING LIKE THAT HAD EVER HAPPENED BEFORE!

THE FATES WERE BESIDE THEMSELVES! HADES WAS FLIPPING HIS LID!

AND ZEUS...

ASKLEPIOS HAS UPSET THE NATURAL ORDER OF THE COSMOS.

HE HAS DONE WHAT EVEN APOLLO COULD NOT DO TO SAVE HIS BELOVED HYACINTH.

ASKLEPIOS HAS BROUGHT THE DEAD BACK TO LIFE.

ONLY THE GODS NEVER DIE.

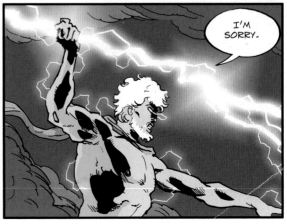

I'M SORRY.

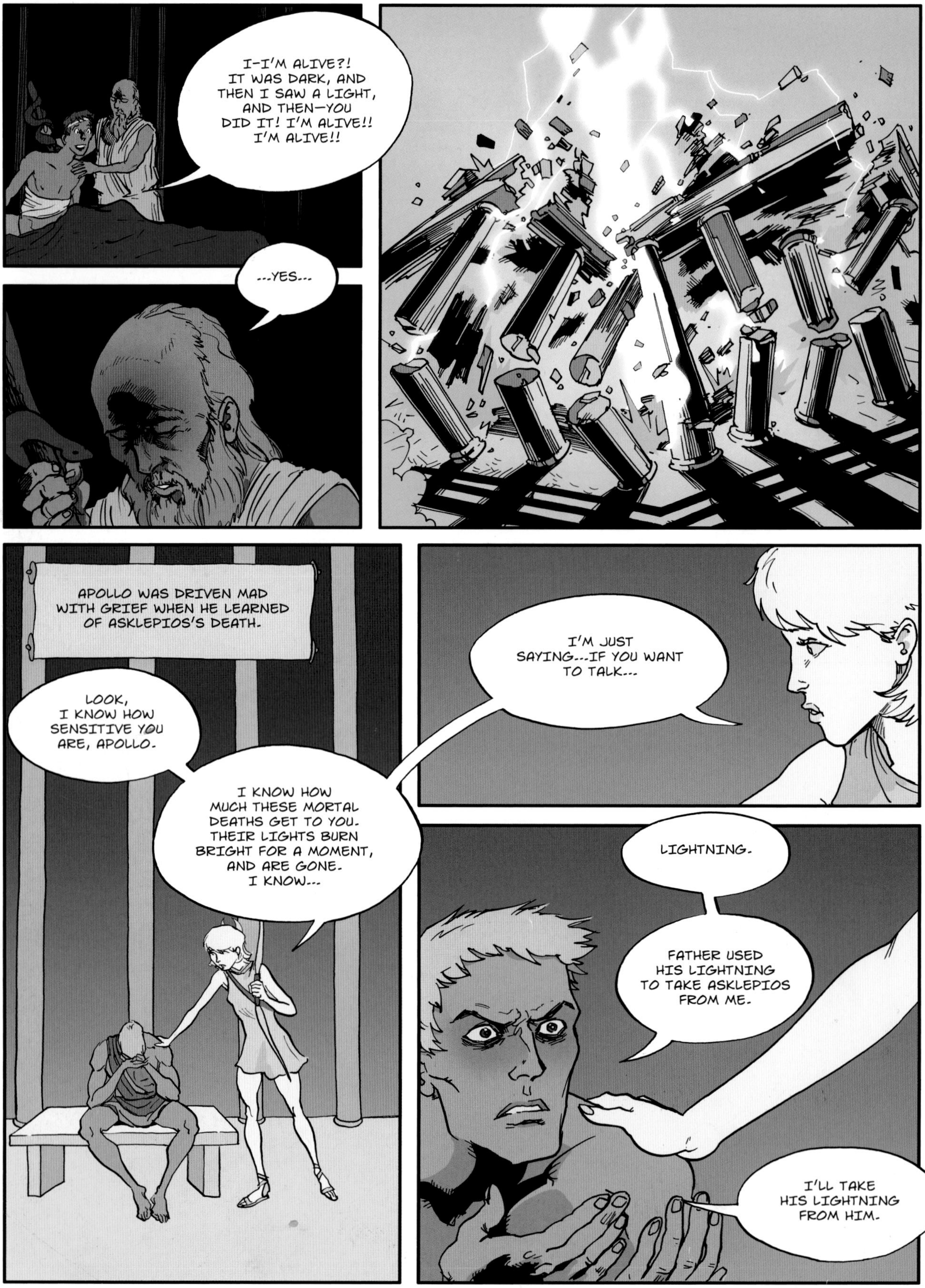
I-I'M ALIVE?! IT WAS DARK, AND THEN I SAW A LIGHT, AND THEN—YOU DID IT! I'M ALIVE!! I'M ALIVE!!
...YES...
APOLLO WAS DRIVEN MAD WITH GRIEF WHEN HE LEARNED OF ASKLEPIOS'S DEATH.
LOOK, I KNOW HOW SENSITIVE YOU ARE, APOLLO.
I KNOW HOW MUCH THESE MORTAL DEATHS GET TO YOU. THEIR LIGHTS BURN BRIGHT FOR A MOMENT, AND ARE GONE. I KNOW...
I'M JUST SAYING...IF YOU WANT TO TALK...
LIGHTNING.
FATHER USED HIS LIGHTNING TO TAKE ASKLEPIOS FROM ME.
I'LL TAKE HIS LIGHTNING FROM HIM.

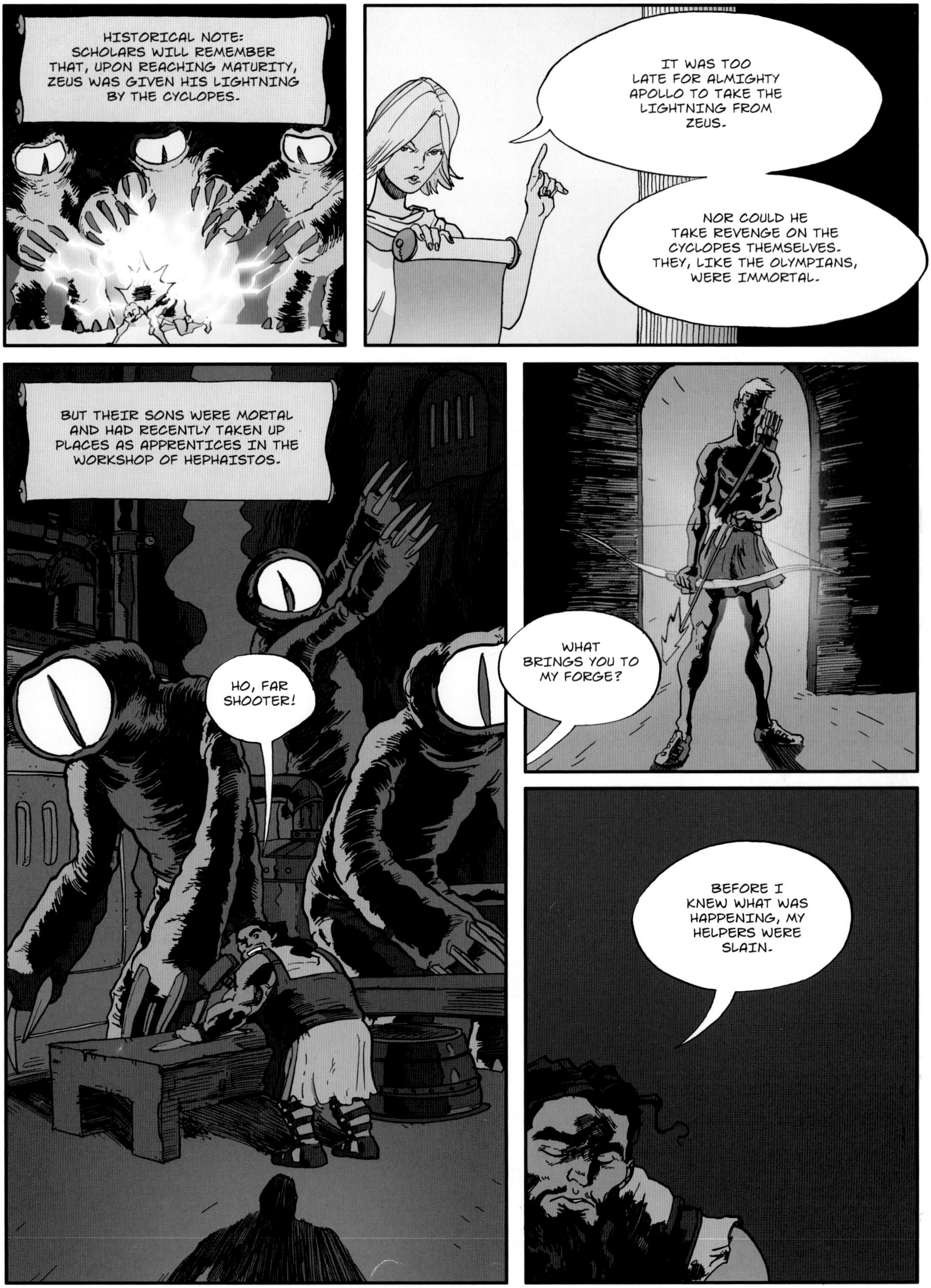

HISTORICAL NOTE: SCHOLARS WILL REMEMBER THAT, UPON REACHING MATURITY, ZEUS WAS GIVEN HIS LIGHTNING BY THE CYCLOPES.
IT WAS TOO LATE FOR ALMIGHTY APOLLO TO TAKE THE LIGHTNING FROM ZEUS.
NOR COULD HE TAKE REVENGE ON THE CYCLOPES THEMSELVES. THEY, LIKE THE OLYMPIANS, WERE IMMORTAL.
BUT THEIR SONS WERE MORTAL AND HAD RECENTLY TAKEN UP PLACES AS APPRENTICES IN THE WORKSHOP OF HEPHAISTOS.
HO, FAR SHOOTER!
WHAT BRINGS YOU TO MY FORGE?
BEFORE I KNEW WHAT WAS HAPPENING, MY HELPERS WERE SLAIN.

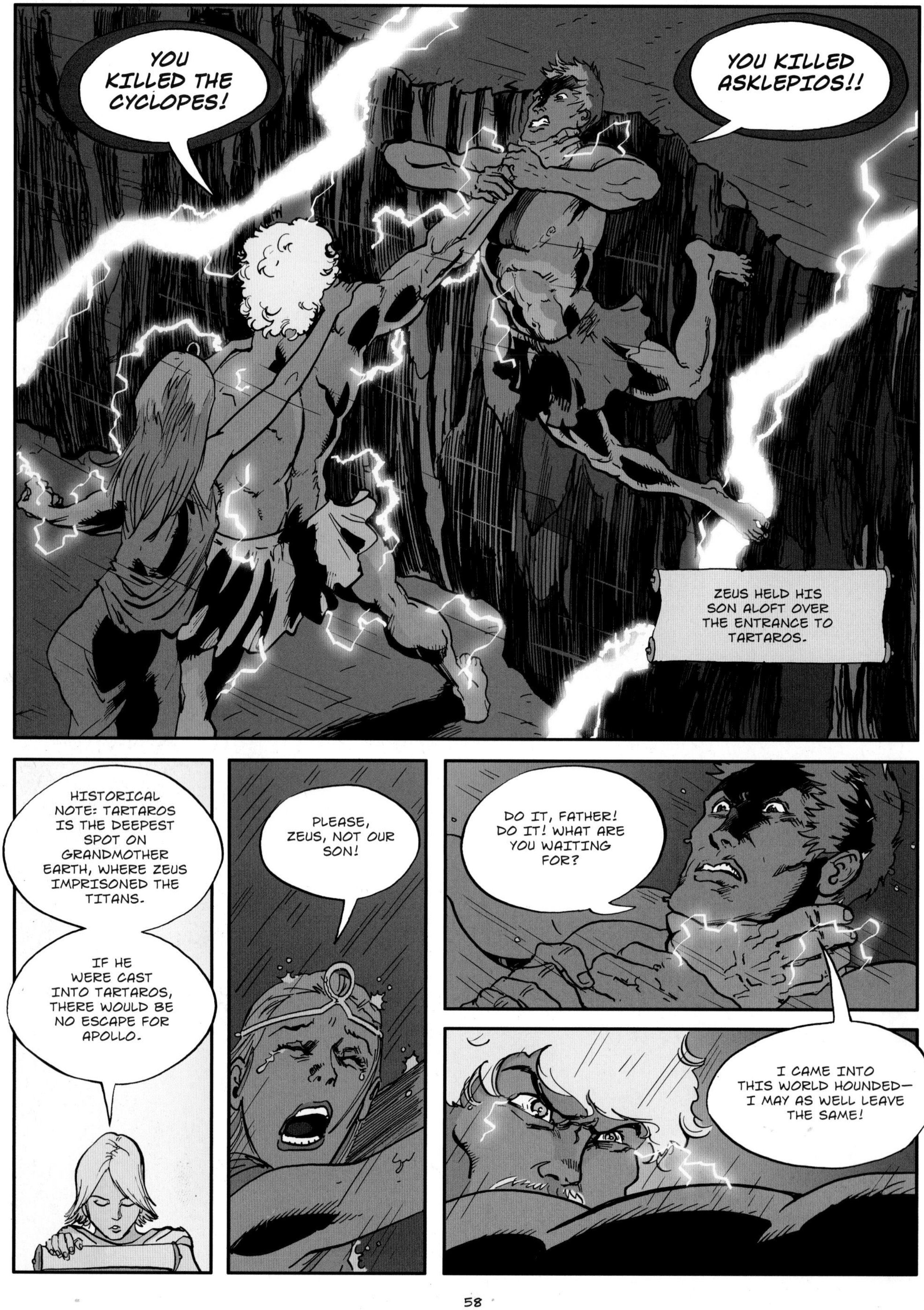
YOU KILLED THE CYCLOPES!
YOU KILLED ASKLEPIOS!!
ZEUS HELD HIS SON ALOFT OVER THE ENTRANCE TO TARTAROS.
HISTORICAL NOTE: TARTAROS IS THE DEEPEST SPOT ON GRANDMOTHER EARTH, WHERE ZEUS IMPRISONED THE TITANS.
IF HE WERE CAST INTO TARTAROS, THERE WOULD BE NO ESCAPE FOR APOLLO.
PLEASE, ZEUS, NOT OUR SON!
DO IT, FATHER! DO IT! WHAT ARE YOU WAITING FOR?
I CAME INTO THIS WORLD HOUNDED— I MAY AS WELL LEAVE THE SAME!

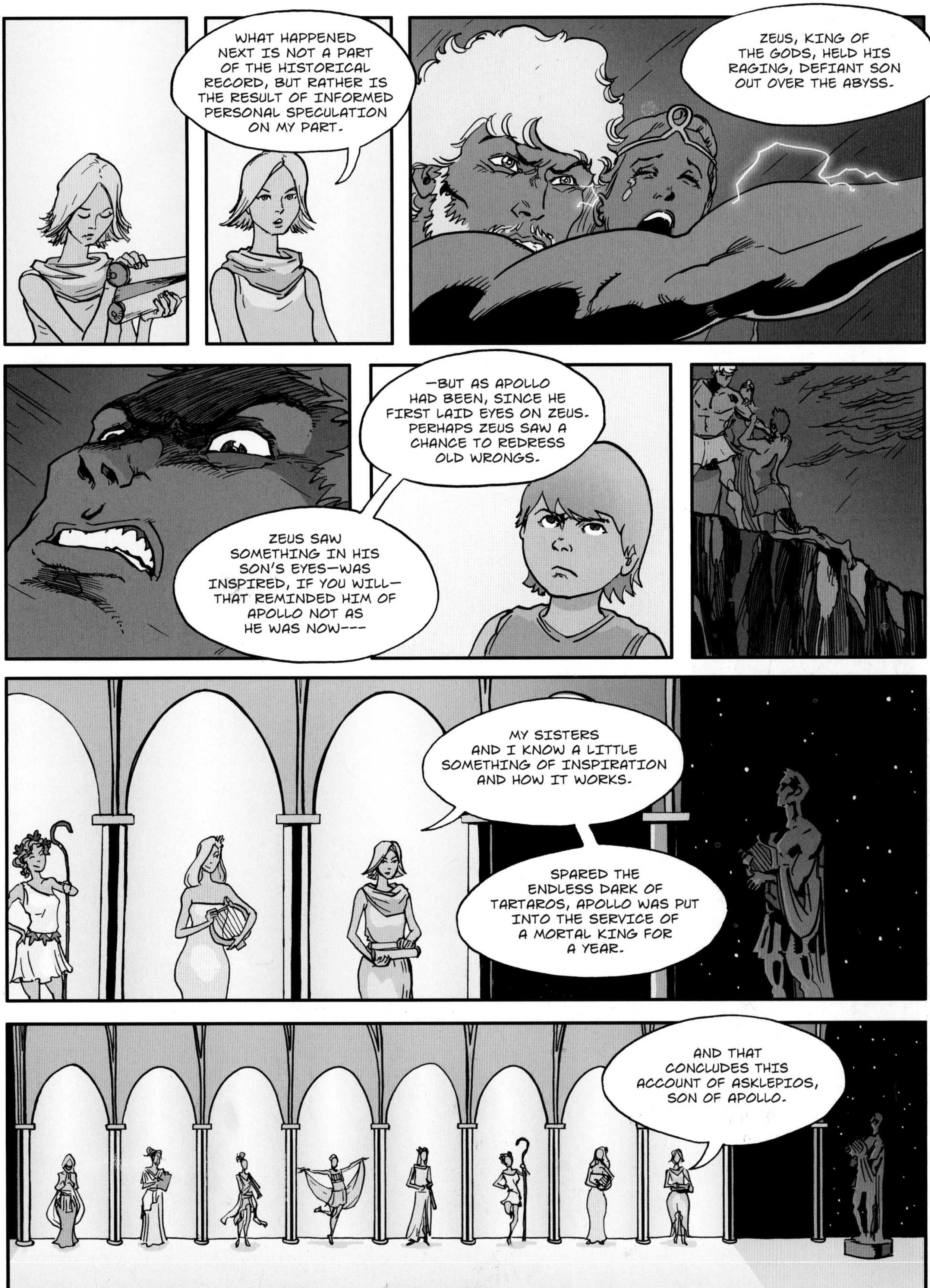
WHAT HAPPENED NEXT IS NOT A PART OF THE HISTORICAL RECORD, BUT RATHER IS THE RESULT OF INFORMED PERSONAL SPECULATION ON MY PART.
ZEUS, KING OF THE GODS, HELD HIS RAGING, DEFIANT SON OUT OVER THE ABYSS.
ZEUS SAW SOMETHING IN HIS SON'S EYES—WAS INSPIRED, IF YOU WILL—THAT REMINDED HIM OF APOLLO NOT AS HE WAS NOW---
—BUT AS APOLLO HAD BEEN, SINCE HE FIRST LAID EYES ON ZEUS. PERHAPS ZEUS SAW A CHANCE TO REDRESS OLD WRONGS.
MY SISTERS AND I KNOW A LITTLE SOMETHING OF INSPIRATION AND HOW IT WORKS.
SPARED THE ENDLESS DARK OF TARTAROS, APOLLO WAS PUT INTO THE SERVICE OF A MORTAL KING FOR A YEAR.
AND THAT CONCLUDES THIS ACCOUNT OF ASKLEPIOS, SON OF APOLLO.

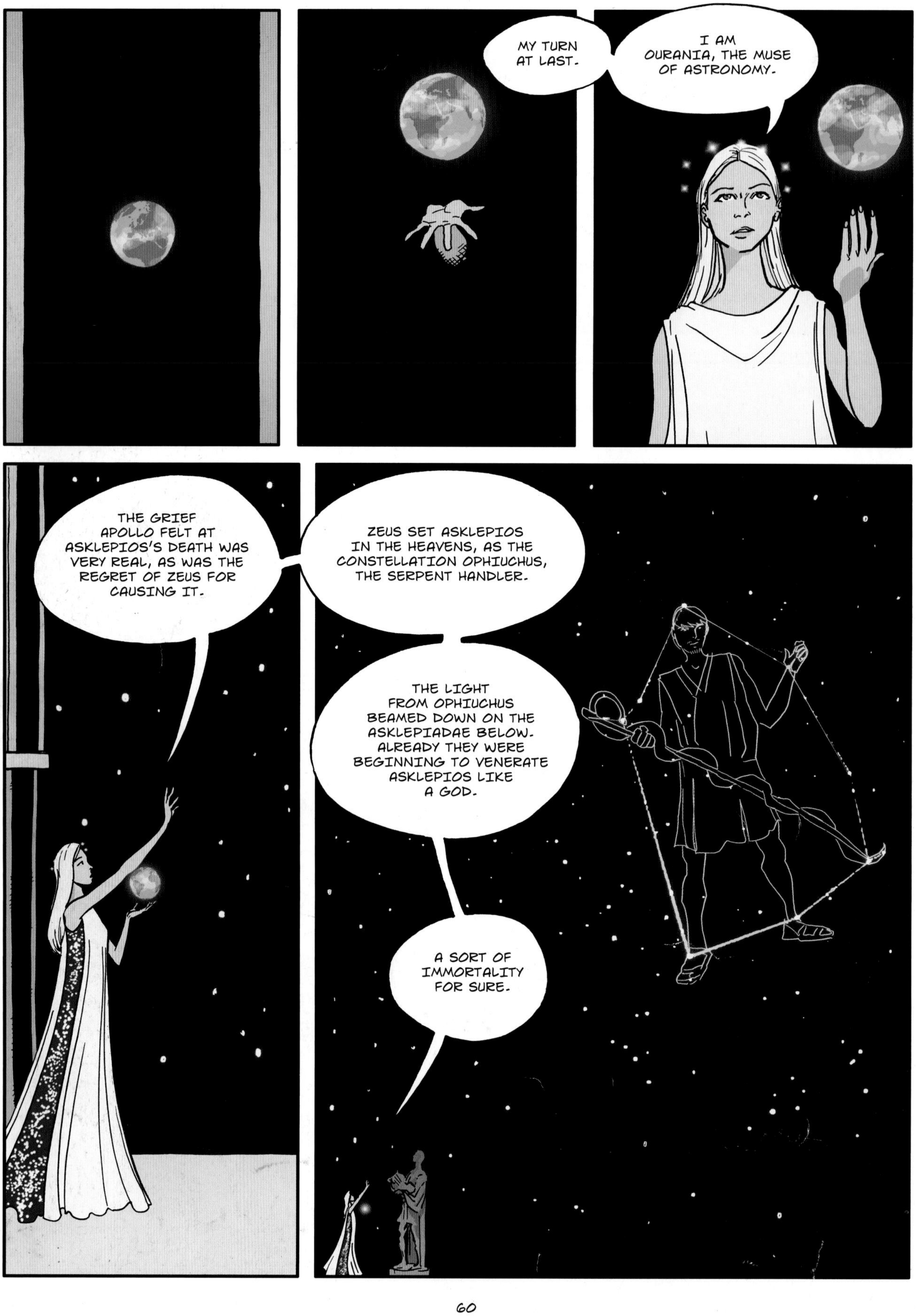

MY TURN AT LAST.
I AM OURANIA, THE MUSE OF ASTRONOMY.
THE GRIEF APOLLO FELT AT ASKLEPIOS'S DEATH WAS VERY REAL, AS WAS THE REGRET OF ZEUS FOR CAUSING IT.
ZEUS SET ASKLEPIOS IN THE HEAVENS, AS THE CONSTELLATION OPHIUCHUS, THE SERPENT HANDLER.
THE LIGHT FROM OPHIUCHUS BEAMED DOWN ON THE ASKLEPIADAE BELOW. ALREADY THEY WERE BEGINNING TO VENERATE ASKLEPIOS LIKE A GOD.
A SORT OF IMMORTALITY FOR SURE.

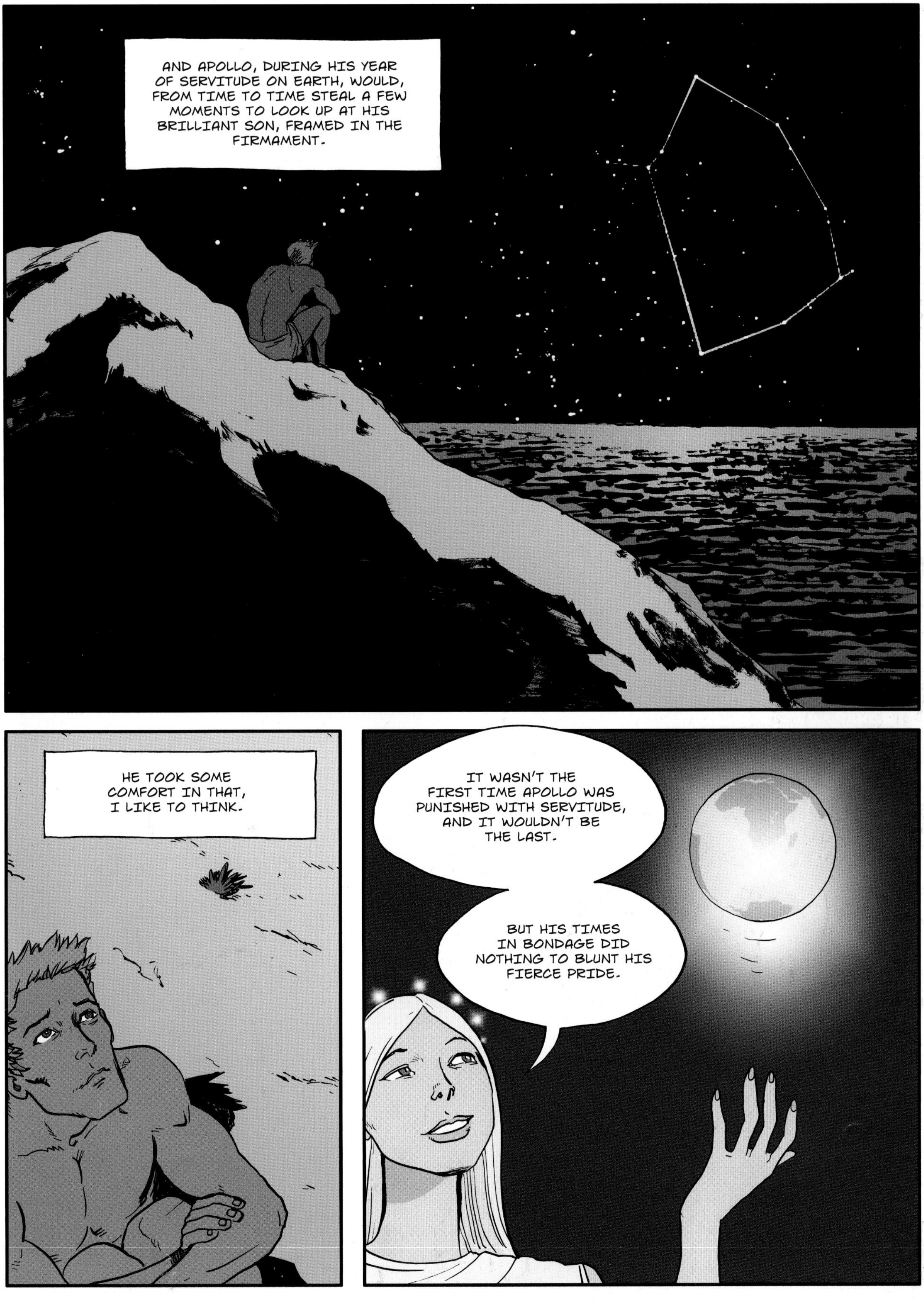
AND APOLLO, DURING HIS YEAR OF SERVITUDE ON EARTH, WOULD, FROM TIME TO TIME STEAL A FEW MOMENTS TO LOOK UP AT HIS BRILLIANT SON, FRAMED IN THE FIRMAMENT.
HE TOOK SOME COMFORT IN THAT, I LIKE TO THINK.
IT WASN'T THE FIRST TIME APOLLO WAS PUNISHED WITH SERVITUDE, AND IT WOULDN'T BE THE LAST.
BUT HIS TIMES IN BONDAGE DID NOTHING TO BLUNT HIS FIERCE PRIDE.

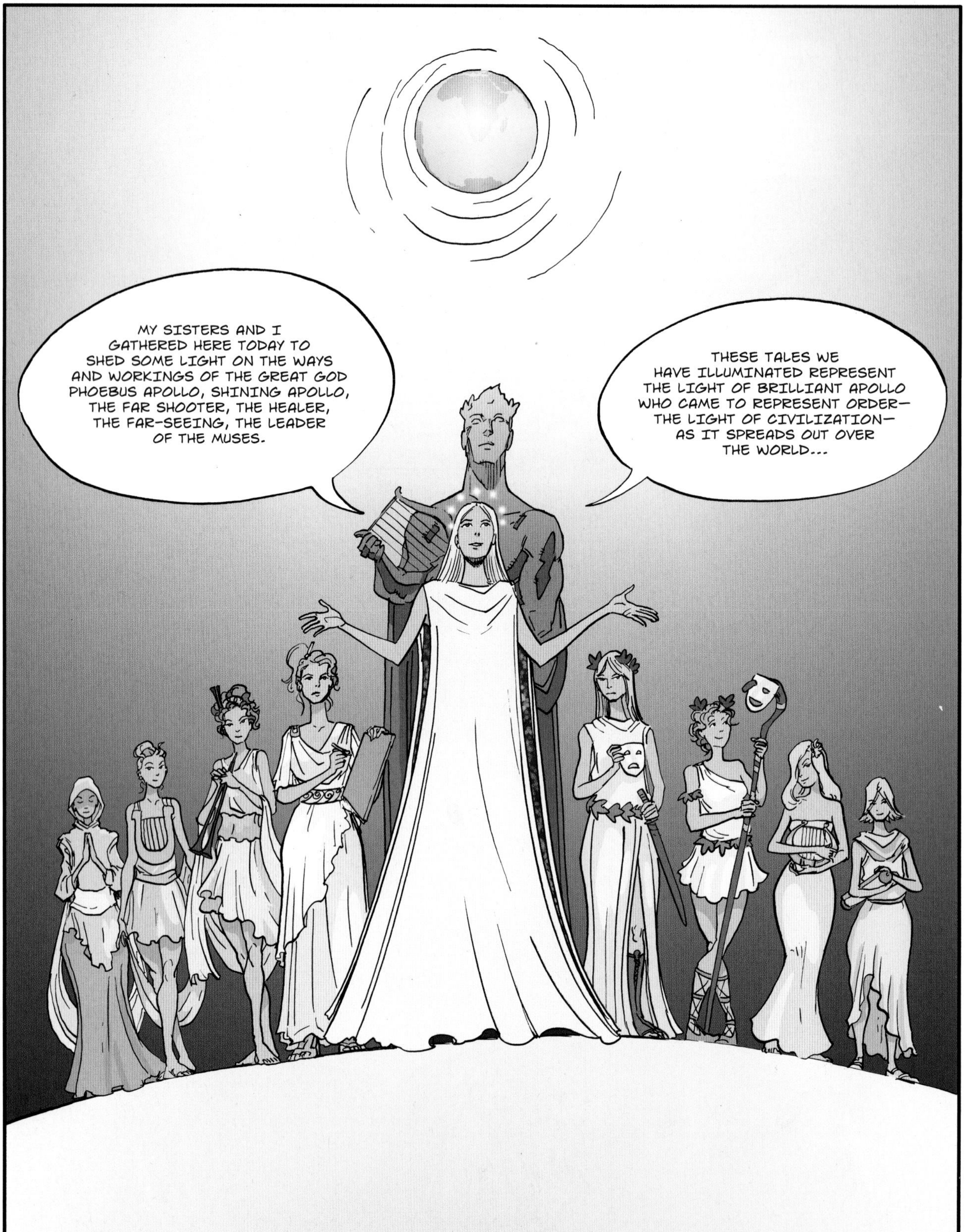
MY SISTERS AND I GATHERED HERE TODAY TO SHED SOME LIGHT ON THE WAYS AND WORKINGS OF THE GREAT GOD PHOEBUS APOLLO, SHINING APOLLO, THE FAR SHOOTER, THE HEALER, THE FAR-SEEING, THE LEADER OF THE MUSES.
THESE TALES WE HAVE ILLUMINATED REPRESENT THE LIGHT OF BRILLIANT APOLLO WHO CAME TO REPRESENT ORDER— THE LIGHT OF CIVILIZATION— AS IT SPREADS OUT OVER THE WORLD...

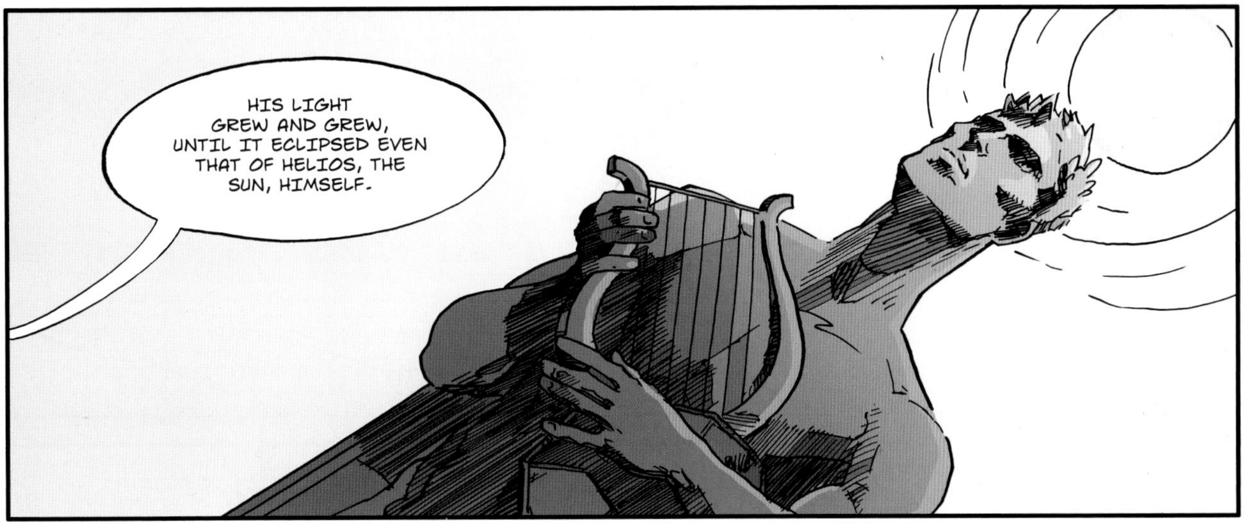
HIS LIGHT GREW AND GREW, UNTIL IT ECLIPSED EVEN THAT OF HELIOS, THE SUN, HIMSELF.

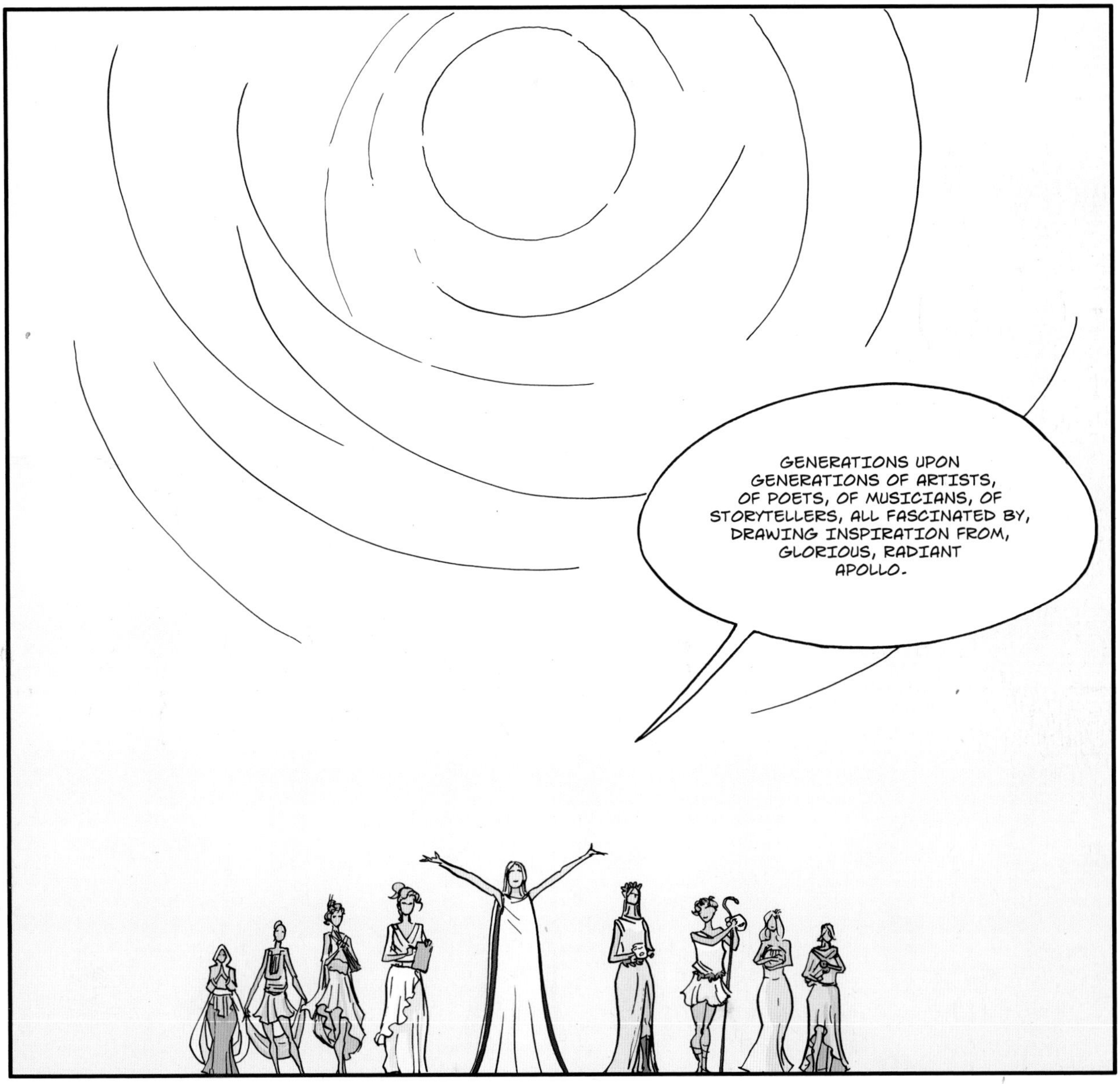
GENERATIONS UPON GENERATIONS OF ARTISTS, OF POETS, OF MUSICIANS, OF STORYTELLERS, ALL FASCINATED BY, DRAWING INSPIRATION FROM, GLORIOUS, RADIANT APOLLO.

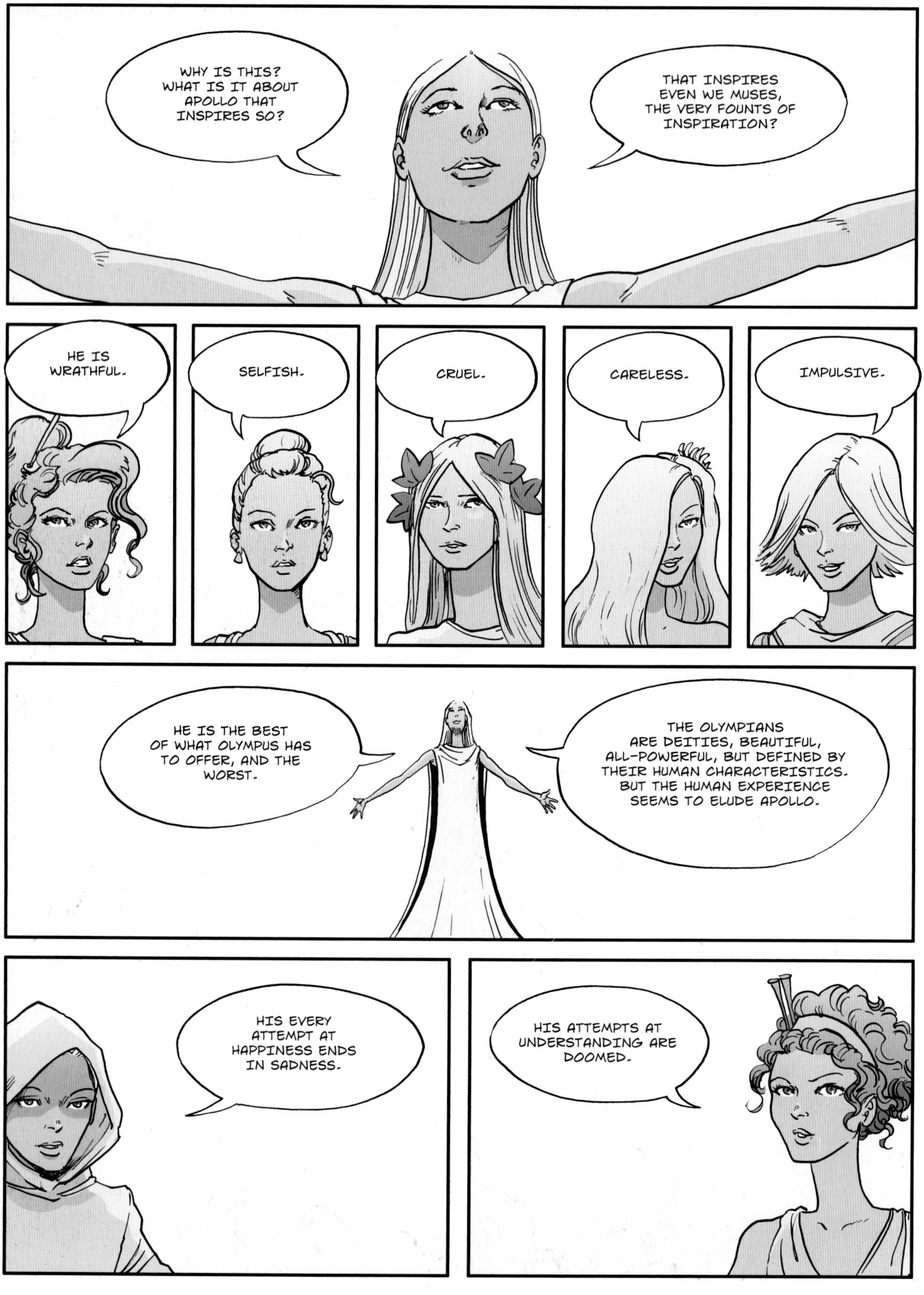
WHY IS THIS? WHAT IS IT ABOUT APOLLO THAT INSPIRES SO?
THAT INSPIRES EVEN WE MUSES, THE VERY FOUNTS OF INSPIRATION?
HE IS WRATHFUL.
SELFISH.
CRUEL.
CARELESS.
IMPULSIVE.
HE IS THE BEST OF WHAT OLYMPUS HAS TO OFFER, AND THE WORST.
THE OLYMPIANS ARE DEITIES, BEAUTIFUL, ALL-POWERFUL, BUT DEFINED BY THEIR HUMAN CHARACTERISTICS. BUT THE HUMAN EXPERIENCE SEEMS TO ELUDE APOLLO.
HIS EVERY ATTEMPT AT HAPPINESS ENDS IN SADNESS.
HIS ATTEMPTS AT UNDERSTANDING ARE DOOMED.

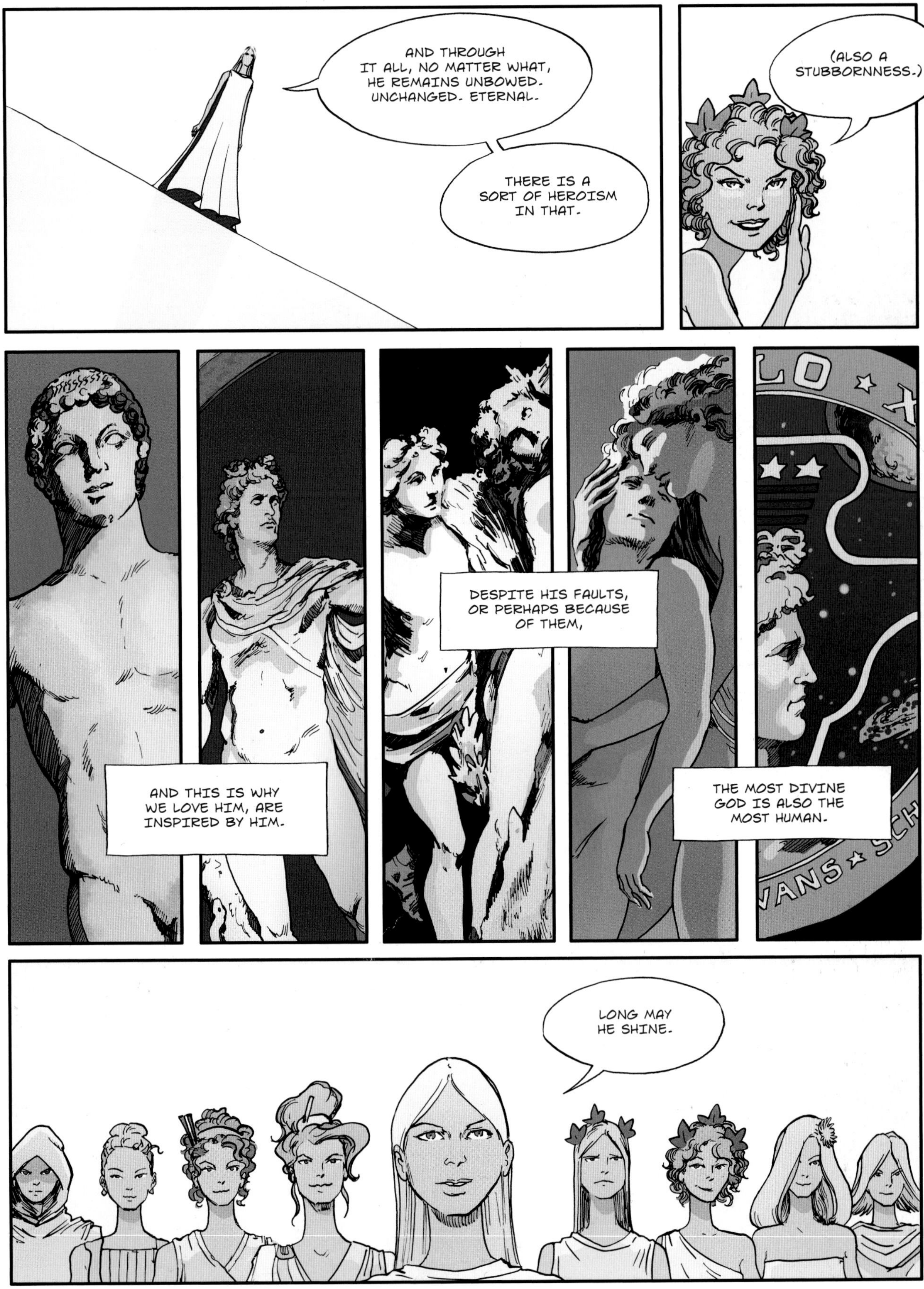
AND THROUGH IT ALL, NO MATTER WHAT, HE REMAINS UNBOWED. UNCHANGED. ETERNAL.
THERE IS A SORT OF HEROISM IN THAT.
(ALSO A STUBBORNNESS.)
AND THIS IS WHY WE LOVE HIM, ARE INSPIRED BY HIM.
DESPITE HIS FAULTS, OR PERHAPS BECAUSE OF THEM,
THE MOST DIVINE GOD IS ALSO THE MOST HUMAN.
LO
VANS
SCH
LONG MAY HE SHINE.

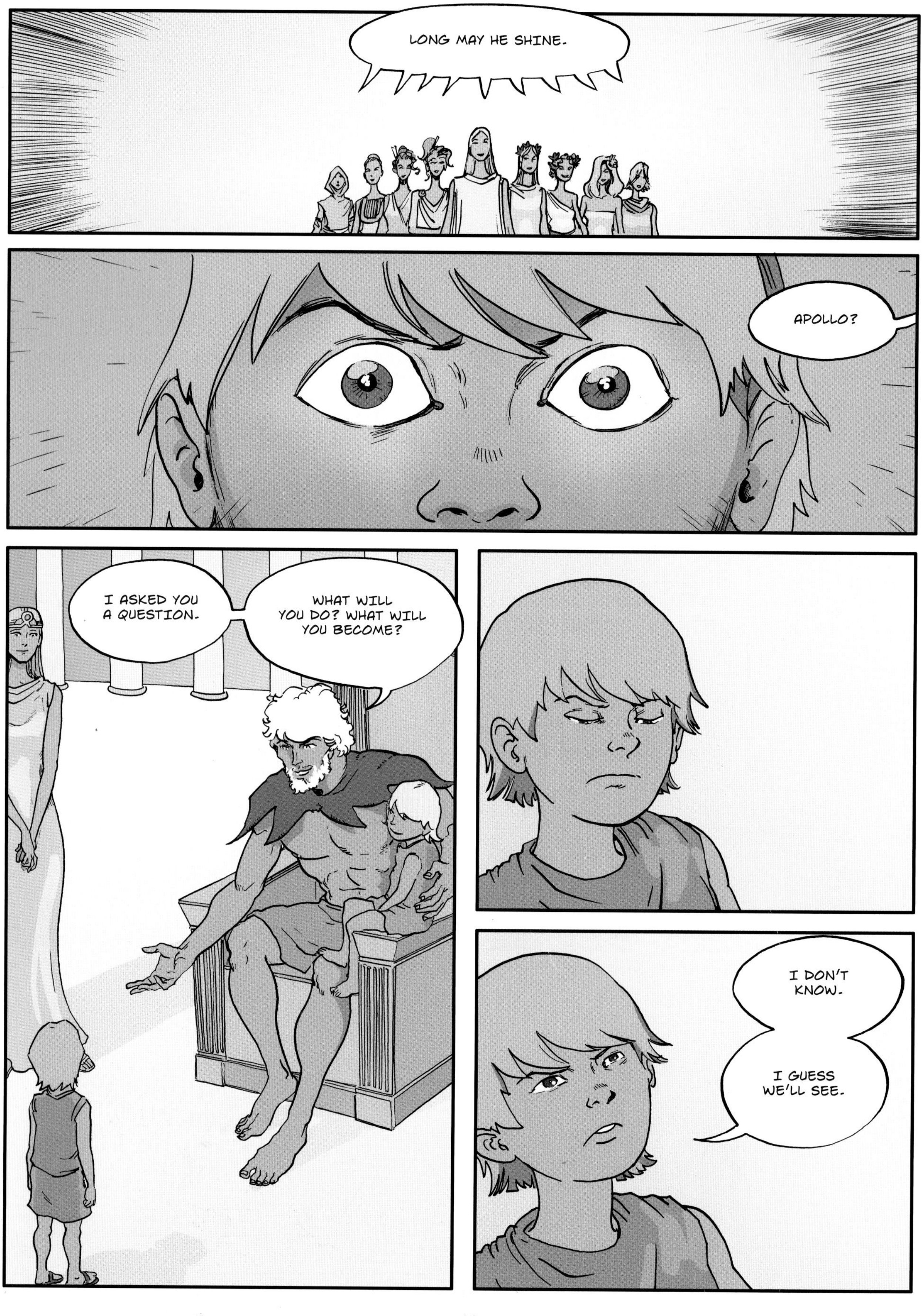
LONG MAY HE SHINE.
APOLLO?
I ASKED YOU A QUESTION.
WHAT WILL YOU DO? WHAT WILL YOU BECOME?
I DON'T KNOW.
I GUESS WE'LL SEE.

# AUTHOR'S NOTE

It's funny that, in a book narrated by the goddesses of inspiration, I've no idea what to write in this author's note.

It's not that I don't have anything to say about Apollo—in fact, I find him to be a fascinating character. Often called the "most Greek" of the Greek Gods, he was beloved by his worshippers in antiquity, yet, and after reading this volume I'm sure you'll agree, he kind of behaves like a monster in most of his stories. It's hard to get behind a god who skins a poor schlub like Marsyas alive for daring to compare himself to him. And woe betide those who become the beloved of Apollo. They may die accidentally (Hyacinth) or deliberately (Koronis), but it's probably not a happy ending either way. No wonder Daphne chose life as a tree rather than as the wife of Apollo.

Way back when, as I was creating the outline for this series, the inspiration for this book was already in place. Before the titling convention of OLYMPIANS was established, this volume was going to be called *Nine Short Stories About Apollo*. Nine stories, each narrated by one of the Mousai, in the style of writing most closely associated with the particular Muse. Easier said than done, certainly—in execution, the nine stories pared down to seven, more or less (a handful of the Mousai doubled up for their tales). In the retelling of all these stories, I encountered again and again the problem of Apollo behaving poorly. I felt I had to find the thread of what made Apollo compelling, not just as the central character of this book, but as a widely revered god in the ancient world.

Ultimately, inspiration did strike—the nature of the stories told about Apollo is exactly what makes him so interesting to others and to me. He is not some bland, perfect deity; he is conflicted, malicious, and spiteful. He is unknowable in his inhumanity, yet simultaneously relatable. Through research and immersion, the personality of shining Apollo revealed itself to me: an imperfect, proud, brilliant god, resplendent in his glory and unashamed of his pettiness. I state as much in the text, through the mouthpieces of the Mousai—was it me speaking through the Muses or the Muses speaking through me?

Inspiration is funny like that. Sometimes you just have to open your mouth, or mind, and let it flow out.

George O'Connor
Brooklyn, NY
2014

# APOLLO
## "SHINING" APOLLO

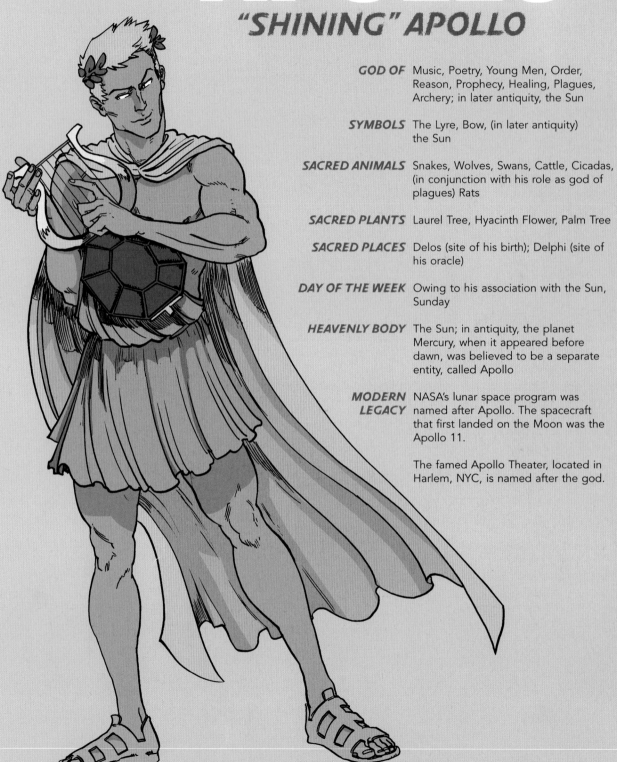

**GOD OF** Music, Poetry, Young Men, Order, Reason, Prophecy, Healing, Plagues, Archery; in later antiquity, the Sun

**SYMBOLS** The Lyre, Bow, (in later antiquity) the Sun

**SACRED ANIMALS** Snakes, Wolves, Swans, Cattle, Cicadas, (in conjunction with his role as god of plagues) Rats

**SACRED PLANTS** Laurel Tree, Hyacinth Flower, Palm Tree

**SACRED PLACES** Delos (site of his birth); Delphi (site of his oracle)

**DAY OF THE WEEK** Owing to his association with the Sun, Sunday

**HEAVENLY BODY** The Sun; in antiquity, the planet Mercury, when it appeared before dawn, was believed to be a separate entity, called Apollo

**MODERN LEGACY** NASA's lunar space program was named after Apollo. The spacecraft that first landed on the Moon was the Apollo 11.

The famed Apollo Theater, located in Harlem, NYC, is named after the god.

# ASKLEPIOS
## THE GREATEST HEALER

**GOD OF**  The Medical Arts

**SYMBOLS**  The serpent-entwined staff known as the Rod of Asklepios

**SACRED ANIMALS**  Aesculapian Snakes, Crows

**SACRED PLACES**  Kos (site of the first Asklepion), Thessaly (his homeland)

**HEAVENLY BODY**  The constellation Ophiuchus

**MODERN LEGACY**  The Rod of Asklepios is still widely used as a symbol for medicine and health care in the modern world.

# GᴿEEK NOTES

PAGE 1: This is a translation of the opening line of *The Odyssey*. There are a lot of different transliterations of this line floating out there, but this one matched the best my general plea to the Muses for inspiration.

PAGE 4, PANEL 2: Polyhymnia means "many hymns," and as the Muse of Religious Hymns, her story is appropriately told in the form of a religious hymn to Apollo.

PAGE 4, PANEL 3: This line is a reference to earlier in Greek religion. Before the establishment of the canonical nine Muses, there were only three: Melete (Meditation), Mneme (Memory), and Aoede (Song).

PAGE 4, PANEL 6: Hyperborea literally means "beyond the North wind." The stories of Robert E. Howard's famous barbarian character, Conan, take place in the similarly named mythical prehistoric land of The Hyborian Age.

PAGE 6, PANEL 5: Zeus eventually will get his own messenger, with the birth of his son Hermes.

PAGE 9, PANEL 3: In some sources, Eileithyia is not just a title of Hera, but is also her daughter, a separate deity. This separate Eileithyia has no real distinct personality in myth, so I use the Hera-in-one.

PAGE 10, PANEL 4: I sneak this line into every volume of OLYMPIANS, and I'm the only one who cares! But I keep doing it anyway! Why? Who knows? Hahahahaha!

PAGE 11, PANEL 3: Good question. Can I get back to you on this?

PAGE 13, PANEL 6: Kalliope is writing her own name here. She lends her name to the musical instrument the calliope, and, as the Muse of Epic Poetry, she relates the suitably epic story of Apollo and Python. Prominent components of epic poetry are the repeated use of honorific titles and lots of monologues.

PAGE 15: I cccertainly mussst sssay I surely sssavored ssscripting the sssinissster sssibilance of the ssslithering ssserpent Python.

PAGE 15, PANEL 6: Ooh, burn!

PAGES 18–19: This is why one of Apollo's cult titles was Apollo Hekateros, or Apollo of the hundred arrows.

PAGE 21, PANEL 2: Ooh, burn!

PAGE 23: All of Euterpe's dialogue is written in iambic pentameter; all of Terpsichore's dialogue is written in the form of a rhyming Greek-chorus response. I tell you this so that you can nod appreciatively whilst stroking your chin and say to yourself, "My, this O'Connor chap certainly is a sharp fellow, and that's no lie." You're probably wearing a tweed jacket and blowing bubbles with a pipe, too.

PAGE 23, PANEL 3: I've said it before, and I'll say it again: Eros is a little punk.

PAGE 30, PANEL 3: Apollo's line here is continuing the iambic pentameter scheme from Euterpe's earlier lines of narration. Again, my, what a sharp fellow I am.

PAGE 31, PANEL 2: The mask symbols of Thalia (not to be confused with the Charite of the same name) and Melpomene are still used to this day to denote the theater.

PAGE 31, PANEL 6: This layout here borrows its composition from the painting *Le dejeuner sur l'herbe*, or *The Luncheon on the Grass*, by Edouard Manet, which in turn borrowed its composition from a detail of an engraving by Marcantonio Raimondi and Raphael (the artist, not the teenage mutant ninja turtle) called *The Judgment of Paris*.

PAGE 32, PANEL 3: He did, and that is a tale for another day.

PAGE 32, PANEL 8: If you've ever seen an old-timey cartoon where someone who has no business being on stage is yanked off stage by a big hook, you now know where that comes from—the shepherd's staff of Thalia.

PAGE 33, PANEL 7: Often viewed as a later addition to Mount Olympus, I've not yet had much of a chance to spotlight Dionysos in OLYMPIANS until this point. I was very excited to have the opportunity to finally bring the god of revelry fully into the fold.

PAGE 35, PANEL 5: Dionysos and Apollo have been famously compared and contrasted by Nietzsche and others: Dionysos represents the Dionysian, chaotic and emotional, whereas Apollo represents the Apollonian, logical and rational. I think that Apollo and Dionysos, as half-brothers, would be civil to each other, but secretly would not be able to stand each other. I hope I conveyed that successfully here.

PAGE 38, PANEL 5: Gulp is right.

PAGE 41: Erato, as Muse of Love Poetry, tells her tale in a poem based on the style of the famous Greek poet Sappho, famous for her erotic poetry. Plato famously called Sappho the tenth Muse.

PAGE 42, PANEL 1: We first met Zephyros in OLYMPIANS Book 6, *Aphrodite: Goddess of Love*. It was Zephyros that initially spotted Aphrodite as she first came ashore at Cyprus. The composition of this panel is based on a famous ancient Greek dish painting.

PAGE 43, PANEL 5: As Muse of Mimicry, Erato performs portions of the story in mime because, y'know, I'm such a clever fellow. I was going to make a joke here about Erato being trapped in an invisible box, but man, even I have standards.

PAGE 47, PANEL 1: That's the figure of Hermes zipping away behind Apollo. As shown elsewhere in the series— most prominently in OLYMPIANS Book 4, *Hades: Lord of the Dead*—Hermes arrives at the moment of death and spirits the shade of the recently deceased to the Underworld.

PAGE 48, PANEL 5: Boy, that's the truth. Not a lot of happy endings for loves of Apollo. Now you know why Demeter freaks out when Apollo is crushing on Kore (Persephone) in the aforementioned OLYMPIANS Book 4, *Hades: Lord of the Dead*.

PAGE 49: As Muse of History, Clio delivers her tale in a documentary style, complete with talking-head interviews of principal players. (We get it, George—you're so clever!)

PAGE 51, PANEL 5: Asklepios's name means "to cut open," in reference to his unusual birth.

PAGE 52, PANEL 8: The staff of Asklepios is still widely used in the world today as a symbol of medicine. In many places, however, the staff of Asklepios has been replaced by the also-snake-entwined wand of Hermes. While this appears to have been done accidentally, I say Hermes the trickster did it on purpose.

PAGE 53, PANEL 1: Hygeia lends her name to the word and concept of hygiene; Panacea, whose name means "cure all," has also seen her name become a word, meaning, appropriately, a cure-all.

PAGE 53, PANEL 5: The apotheosis of Heracles was seen in OLYMPIANS Book 3, *Hera: The Goddess and Her Glory*.

PAGE 54, PANEL 2: We've seen Theseus in this hallway before, in OLYMPIANS Book 5, *Poseidon: Earth Shaker*.

PAGE 54, PANEL 4: There's that Hermes again.

PAGE 60, PANEL 5: Asklepios was venerated throughout ancient Greece as a deity, but myth holds that he died by Zeus's hand. The constellation seems to have been a suitable explanation for how he still existed in some form despite having met his mortal end.

PAGE 65, PANELS 3–7: This is a montage of great works of mankind inspired by Apollo. From left to right, they are: *The Strangford Apollo*, an archaic Greek *kouros* from the 5th century BCE; *Apollo Belvedere*, a marble statue from the classical period; Bernini's *Apollo and Daphne*, a sculpture from the Baroque period; *The Death of Hyacinthos*, an 1801 painting by Jean Broc; and, finally, the emblem for Apollo 17, the final mission in the United States's lunar space program. I chose the emblem for Apollo 17 in particular because it so prominently featured an image of Apollo, but I must say that I went back and forth about including so modern a representation of the god in this list. Ultimately I decided yes, because, as the god of prognostication, it only made sense to include the future (and besides, both the Bernini and Broc pieces are from the future as well), and there are few things more inspiring than humanity's trip to the moon.

PAGE 66, PANEL 3: There's that question again...

# THE MOUSAI
## THE GODDESSES OF INSPIRATION

POLYHYMNIA    ERATO    MELPOMENE    THALIA

***ROMAN NAME*** The Muses

***INDIVIDUAL NAMES, ROLES, AND SYMBOLS*** Kalliope (Muse of Epic Poetry, Stylus and Tablet), Ourania (Astronomy, Globe), Euterpe (Lyric Poetry and Music, Double Flute), Terpsichore (Choral Song and Dance, Plectrum and Lyre), Polyhymnia (Religious Hymns, Pensive Stance and Veil), Thalia (Comedy, Shepherd's Staff and Smiling Mask), Melpomene (Tragedy, Sword and Sad Mask), Clio (History, Scroll), and Erato (Love Poetry and Mimicry, Lyre)

***SACRED PLACES*** Mount Helikon, Boiotia (early site of cult), Delphi (where they were worshipped alongside Apollo)

***MODERN LEGACY*** Modern words such as "music" and "museum" are derived from these goddesses.

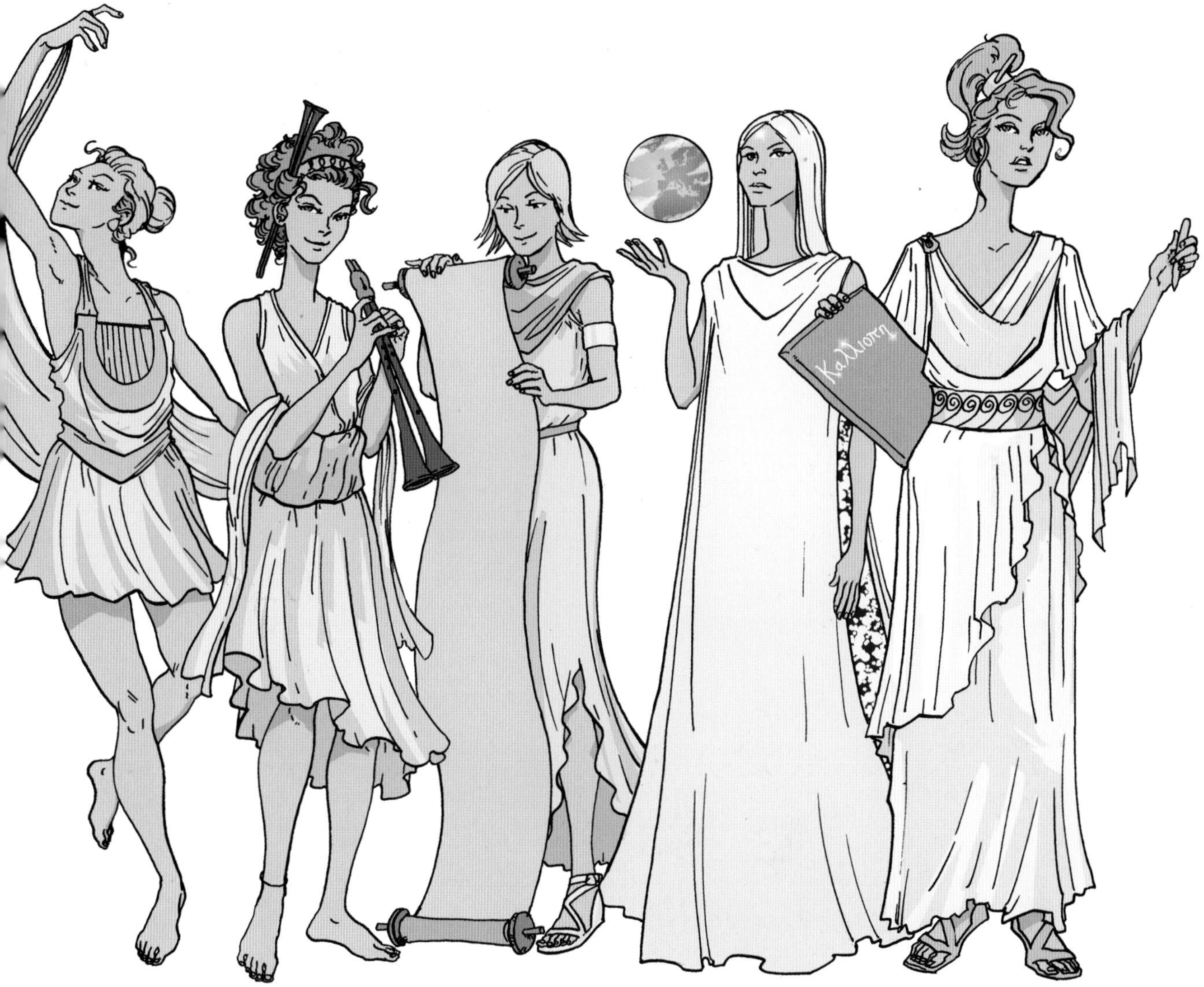
Καλλιοπη

***TERPSICHORE*** ***EUTERPE*** ***CLIO*** ***OURANIA*** ***KALLIOPE***

# ABOUT THIS BOOK

**APOLLO: THE BRILLIANT ONE** is the eighth book in OLYMPIANS,
a graphic novel series from First Second that retells the Greek myths.

# FOR DISCUSSION

**1** Apollo is the god of prophecy. If you could tell the future, what would you do?

**2** This book is narrated by the nine Muses, and each of the Muses specializes in a specific art form. Who would be some good modern-day additions to the ranks of the Mousai?

**3** Apollo is very unlucky in love. Heck, Daphne would rather be a tree than be with him! Why do you think that is?

**4** Do you think Apollo was fair in what he did to Marsyas? Was Marsyas smart to challenge Apollo? What would you ask for if you won a competition with Apollo?

**5** Do you think Zeus was right to kill Asklepios when Asklepios brought a man back to life? Was Apollo right to kill the Cyclopes's sons as revenge?

**6** Apollo was not originally a sun god. Why do you think he became associated with the sun?

**7** Why do you think the mission to go to the moon was named after Apollo instead of Artemis?

**8** Very few people believe in the Greek gods today. Why do you think it's important that we still learn about them?

# BIBLIOGRAPHY

*HESIOD: VOLUME 1, THEOGENY. WORKS AND DAYS: TESTIMONIA.*
**EDITED AND TRANSLATED BY GLENN W MOST. LOEB CLASSICAL LIBRARY. CAMBRIDGE, MA: HARVARD UNIVERSITY PRESS, 2007.**
Lots of cool snippets about Apollo himself to be found here, but I've also used this is as the source for the nine canonical Muses. Hesiod is the foundation upon which OLYMPIANS has been constructed.

*AELIAN: HISTORICAL MISCELLANY.*
**TRANSLATED BY NIGEL G WILSON. LOEB CLASSICAL LIBRARY. CAMBRIDGE, MA: HARVARD UNIVERSITY PRESS, 1997.**
That one weird little detail from the story of Marsyas, that his skin dances for flutes but stays still for lyres, comes from this book. Hilarious!

*HOMERIC HYMNS. HOMERIC APOCRYPHA. LIVES OF HOMER.*
**EDITED AND TRANSLATED BY M L WEST. LOEB CLASSICAL LIBRARY. CAMBRIDGE, MA: HARVARD UNIVERSITY PRESS, 2007.**
I used the Homeric Hymn to Apollo contained within this collection as a source for the birth of Apollo and his slaying of the serpent Python.

*METAMORPHOSES.* **OVID. TRANSLATED BY DAVID RAEBURN. NEW YORK: PENGUIN CLASSICS, 2004.**
I used this as the primary account for my retellings of both Daphne and Hyacinth. *Metamorphoses* is a Roman text, so normally I note that the gods' names are their Roman equivalents, but Apollo is the same in Greek and Roman. Score!

*THEOI GREEK MYTHOLOGY WEB SITE* **WWW.THEOI.COM**
Without a doubt, the single most valuable resource I came across in this entire venture. At Theoi.com, you can find an encyclopedia of various gods and goddesses from Greek mythology, cross referenced with every mention of them they could find in literally hundreds of ancient Greek and Roman texts. Unfortunately, it's not quite complete, and it doesn't seem to be updated anymore.

**WWW.LIBRARY.THEOI.COM**
A subsection of the above site, it's an online archive of hundreds of ancient Greek and Roman texts. Many of these have never been published in the traditional sense, and many are just fragments recovered from ancient papyrus, or recovered text from other authors' quotations of lost epics. Invaluable.

*MYTH INDEX WEB SITE* **WWW.MYTHINDEX.COM**
Another mythology Web site connected to Theoi.com. While it doesn't have the painstakingly compiled quotations from ancient texts, it does offer some impressive encyclopedic entries on virtually every character to ever pass through a Greek myth. Pretty amazing.

# ALSO RECOMMENDED
## FOR YOUNGER READERS

*D'Aulaires' Book of Greek Myths*. Ingri and Edgar Parin D'Aulaire. New York: Doubleday, 1962.

## FOR OLDER READERS

*The Marriage of Cadmus and Harmony*. Robert Calasso. New York: Knopf, 1993.

*Mythology*. Edith Hamilton. New York: Grand Central Publishing, 1999.

*For Seth Kushner, 1973–2015, the gifted artist responsible for my author photo. No Hero ever fought so hard and so brave against so terrible a monster as you did. Rest in peace.*

*And a welcome to new Olympians Clio and Daphne. Long may you shine.*

—G.O.

First Second

New York

Copyright © 2016 by George O'Connor

Published by First Second
First Second is an imprint of Roaring Brook Press,
a division of Holtzbrinck Publishing Holdings Limited Partnership
175 Fifth Avenue, New York, New York 10010

Cataloging-in-Publication Data is on file at the Library of Congress

Paperback ISBN: 978-1-62672-015-2
Hardcover ISBN: 978-1-62672-016-9

First Second books may be purchased for business or promotional use.
For information on bulk purchases please contact the Macmillan Corporate
and Premium Sales Department at (800) 221-7945 x5442 or by email at
specialmarkets@macmillan.com.

First Edition 2016

Book design by Rob Steen

Printed in China by Toppan Leefung Printing Ltd., Dongguan City, Guangdong Province

Paperback: 10 9 8 7 6 5 4 3 2 1
Hardcover: 10 9 8 7 6 5 4 3 2 1